Zane
&
Madeline

Willow Winters & Lauren Landish
Wall street journal & usa today bestselling authors

From USA Today bestselling authors, Willow Winters and Lauren Landish, comes a smoking hot standalone romance that'll have you wishing you had your own bad boy next door.

Little Miss Goody-Two-Shoes just moved in next door.
She's a good girl, the kind I want to ruin.

The problem is, she knows I'm bad news.
I've always been trouble.

That's why she keeps pushing me away, even with her curvy body pressed against mine and those soft moans spilling from her lips.

Now that she's my neighbor, it's only a matter of time before I'll have her in my arms and clinging to me the way I need her to.

I may not deserve her,
but I want her more than I've ever wanted anything.

She's not getting away from the bad boy next door.

No part of this publication may be reproduced, stored in a retrieval system, or transmitted in any form or by any means, electronic, mechanical, photocopying, recording, scanning, or otherwise, without the prior written permission of the publisher, except in the case of brief quotations within critical reviews and otherwise as permitted by copyright law.

NOTE: This is a work of fiction. Names, characters, places, and incidents are a product of the author's imagination. Any resemblance to real life is purely coincidental. All characters in this story are 18 or older.

Copyright © 2016, Willow Winters Publishing. All rights reserved.

Prologue

Madeline

I turn on my side and face my window, waiting for him to come into view. I feel so naughty. So needy. This is turning into a bad habit.

I bite my lip as he moves his curtains so he can see me.

Our eyes meet, and the hunger I see in his makes every doubt disappear. I want him, and he wants me. There's nothing wrong about that.

His lips turn up into a sexy smirk as his eyes roam my body. He takes his shirt off, his corded muscles rippling with the movement. He's the epitome of power and sex. His jeans are slung low, and the urge to lick the deep "V" at his hips makes my legs scissor. My hand dips down to my pussy and I love that he sees. I love that he watches me.

"Covers off," he mouths, and I obey. I'm wearing a tank top and a skimpy lace thong. He tilts his head and tsks. A small laugh escapes my lips as a blush creeps into my cheeks. I knew he'd want them off. But tonight I want him to take them off of me.

A few weeks ago I would've given him the finger and yanked my curtains closed. But not tonight, not now that I've become addicted to the inked-up bad boy next door.

"Come over." I whisper my plea, and his eyes heat with desire.

"Get wet for me, peaches." I smile shyly at his command and slowly push my fingers against my clit, massaging small circles over my throbbing nub. My head falls back against my pillow, and a faint moan escapes from my parted mouth. I turn my head to the side and with my eyes half-lidded, I watch him watching me.

"More," he says in a deep, rough voice that makes arousal pool in my core. I make my movements faster and hold his heated gaze. His breath comes in shallow pants, and his hand pushes against the bulge in his jeans. I know he wants me. I want him, too.

"Please," the word tumbles from my mouth as I feel my back bow and a hot tingle take over my body. My eyes close as I almost fall and crash with an intense orgasm, but it escapes me. I'm on edge. I *need* him.

I open my eyes, and he's gone. I bite down on my lip and slow my movements. He'll be here soon. He'll fill me, stretching my walls with his massive cock and thrusting his powerful hips until I'm writhing beneath him and screaming his name.

When did I turn into a slave to his lust? I don't beg. I'm not that kind of girl, but he broke my walls down, and I've learned to love it.

He's bad for me. I know he is, but I still crave him. And now that I've given in, I'm all his. Until he's done with me, anyway. I know it's coming.

This arrangement isn't going to last, but I push the thoughts away and force myself to live in the moment.

For now, I belong to the inked-up bad boy next door.

Chapter 1

Madeline

One Month Before....

"I've never seen so many hot guys in my life!" cries Katie Butler, my partner in crime and childhood friend. We're standing in line outside of Club Dusk, the hottest nightclub in this town. As new residents to Grim Lake, a bustling town nestled in the lush Midwest, we've come to check out the nightlife scene on our last night of freedom. Not that the party scene is *my* scene.

Katie has been adamant all week that we go out and have a good time before we spend the next several years with our noses stuck in a book and stressing about exams. While I agree wholeheartedly with her, I'm just not sure if I want to spend the night with horny guys breathing down my neck.

I make a sour face as I survey the sea of young men standing in line in front of us. "Are you sure we're looking at the same people?" I say loudly over the bass of the music coming from within the club.

Honestly, I don't know what Katie's smoking. I wouldn't give a second glance to any of these dudes even if I was walking down the street, desperate to find a man. And the few that are good-looking, already have a chick on their arms.

Not to mention I'm not here to find a boyfriend, I think to myself. *I'm just here to have a couple of drinks and unload some stress. That's it.*

Despite being the goal of maybe eighty percent of the women in attendance, I have no intention of getting sloppy-ass drunk and winding up in some strange asshole's bed the next morning, not knowing how or why I wound up in it.

Besides, after the way my last relationship ended, a boyfriend is the last thing on my mind.

Just thinking about my ex, Zachery Haynes, makes my stomach tense with a mixture of anger and anxiety. We'd been high school sweethearts who thought we'd be spending the rest of our lives together. Our endgame goals were even aligned. College degrees. High-powered jobs. White picket fence. A full-sized family. The whole nine yards.

That dream shattered when I walked in on Zach getting a blowjob from my high school nemesis, Jenna Stout. Seeing her there on her knees, slurping my boyfriend's dick felt like a spear piercing my heart.

Of course, being the egotistical, narcissistic asshole he was, Zachery tried to make it seem like HE was the victim. It was an accident, he claimed. He didn't mean to do it. It was all Jenna's fault for showing up on his doorstep looking hot as fuck in her cheerleader uniform.

She'd seduced him he said, she'd made his dick hard and made him take it out so she could slurp on it like a fucking cherry popsicle. The ridiculous explanation was more than I could take. I left him and Jenna right then and there to continue their oral session, and I never spoke to the bastard ever again.

I did suffer for it, though.

The whole trauma from Zach's betrayal put me in a deep depression, causing my GPA to fall. And by mid-semester, I was close to failing several of my classes. Luckily, with the help of Katie and my father, I was able to pull myself out of my rut in time enough to get my grades back on track to allow me to qualify to go to one of the best universities in the nation.

It's funny how things turn out.

There was one valuable lesson I'd learned from Zach's betrayal, and that was you could never trust a man.

Fuck a boyfriend, I think to myself. *I'll only enter a relationship when I'm good and ready. And that won't be for a very long time.*

I don't intend on dating until I've graduated and landed my dream job. Then and only then will I give the male species a second chance at regaining my trust. Besides, I certainly won't find Mr. Right in a club full of horny guys just looking for the next girl to fuck.

"I must be blind then," I say. "Or just plain stupid."

Katie tears her eyes away from the object of her affection and scowls at me. I must say Miss Katie's makeup is on point tonight, with false eyelashes that would make a drag queen jealous, rosy blush, glossy pink lipstick and dramatic eye shadow. Her hair isn't too shabby, either, styled into a trendy shoulder-length side bob that shimmers under the street light. A tight red dress that hugs her pear-shaped frame completes her look. "You really need to lighten up, Maddy. We came here to have fun, remember?"

I hold Katie's scowl for a moment before letting out a resigned sigh. "I know, I know, I'm just not looking forward to having a line of horny guys buying me drinks and reading me their lame pick-up lines in hopes that I'll sleep with them."

Katie looks at me like I'm crazy. "If you don't want that, then why the hell did you agree to come clubbing in the first place?"

It's a good question. If my goal is to relieve stress, there are a lot more relaxing things I could do rather than come to a rowdy nightclub... Like enjoy a bubble bath with a chilled glass of wine, or cuddle up on the couch with a good romance book.

The truth is I've been avoiding the opposite sex since Zach's betrayal. Maybe subconsciously I wanted to see what it feels like to be desired again, even if it's by a horny guy looking to land his next lay. Yeah, that had to be it. I wanted a boost of confidence.

At five foot four, with green eyes, long blonde hair and a voluptuous figure, I've gotten enough compliments to know that I'm not bad-looking, maybe even pretty. But Zach's cheating had been a blow to my self-esteem. I mean, if I was so beautiful, why did he feel the need to cheat on me?

Stop it, I tell myself, something I do every time I find myself falling into the trap of internalizing my ex's actions. *Zach cheated because he was a narcissistic asshole that only cared about himself. It had nothing to do with my looks.*

It's a mantra I repeat frequently to keep myself from getting depressed. Lately though, I've been having trouble believing it.

"Are you kidding me?" I demand. "You're really going to act like you weren't bugging me all damn week to come out and have some fun?" I look at her like she's lost her mind. "I think your exact words were, 'Your face is starting to look like cracked asphalt because of the perpetual scowl you've had on your mug for the past month.'"

"You still didn't have to come," says Katie defensively. "And your face *was* starting to look like cracked asphalt."

I roll my eyes. "Get real. If I hadn't come I would've never heard the end of it." I put my finger to my lips and make a thoughtful expression. "Hmm, what was one of the arguments you were using to blackmail me to be your partner in crime? Oh yeah, that's right, 'I'm going to be so pissed off at you Maddy, if you don't come get shitfaced with me before we move into our new condo together.'"

"I did not say that."

I glower. "Yes, you did."

Placing her hands on her hips, Katie scowls back at me and admits, "Okay, maybe I did. Now what?"

"Nothing. Just letting it be known that I had no choice in the matter if I didn't want to deal with a pissed off diva for the next couple of weeks."

"I am not a diva!" she wails.

"Tell that to Vanessa! She's the prissiest person I know, and even she knows you're a diva!"

"Vanessa is a cat!" Katie protests.

"That's my point exactly."

"Ugh, whatever. I just don't know why you're giving me so much grief over this. What's so bad about me wanting you to come out and interact with the opposite sex for just one night, huh?"

I fall silent for a moment as the line moves up. We're only a couple of feet from being let inside the club, and I have to admit I'm feeling a little excited. "I don't know," I say finally. "I guess I'm still not over Zach."

Katie shakes her head, her bob swishing to the side. "You're crazy. Why wouldn't you be over that ego-inflated douchebag?"

"I don't mean him per se, I mean what he did."

Katie frowns. "Oh. I understand... but we talked about that, remember? We agreed that Zach was an asshole who never cared about you, you were better off without him, and that you wouldn't let what he'd done bother you anymore."

"I know, Katie, and for a while I didn't let it get to me... but... I... lately I've been feeling like I'll never be able to trust guys again," I confess reluctantly.

"Who says you have to trust a guy to fuck him?" she replies with a shrug.

"Katie!" I object in horror.

Katie makes an innocent face. "Wha?"

"I'm not here to screw!"

"Why not? Your muffin has cobwebs."

I cross my arms over my chest and threaten, "I'm going to leave."

Katie lets out a wild laugh at my exasperation. "I'm just playing! Sort of. You know, just because Zach cheated on you, doesn't mean you can't have a sexual relationship with someone."

"It does in my book. Besides, I'm not one to sleep around."

Katie snorts. "Why sell yourself short? There's nothing wrong with having sex with someone, no strings attached. Then you don't have to deal with all the bullshit that comes with a relationship, like what happened between you and Zach."

Katie has a point. Since Zach, I'd sworn off sex and probably would remain celibate for years to come. Why deny myself the simple pleasures in life because of the actions of one heartless bastard? What harm could come from fulfilling a primal need from time to time?

Because I want it to be special, I tell myself. *If I sleep with a guy just to satisfy an itch, it won't mean anything.*

"If anything," Katie continues while I'm lost in thought, " Zach's betrayal should make you want to use guys and leave them."

"No thanks," I say. "I won't stoop to his level."

"That's not stooping to his level; it's called empowering yourself."

"How is becoming the village slut empowering?"

Katie laughs. "Hey, guys do it all the time, and they're rewarded for it. We do it, and we're sluts. How is that fair?"

"You know I know it's not, but it just doesn't interest me."

"Won't you even consider the possibility?"

"Nope. I'm only here because you made me come... and because I want free cosmopolitans."

Katie giggles. "Don't we all? But seriously, if a smoking hot guy comes up to you and wants to have a little fun, are you really going to turn him down?"

"Yep."

"Liar."

"Just watch me."

I have every intention of keeping my word. I don't care if some guy buys me a dozen free drinks or is a clone of Charlie Hunnam and Channing Tatum put together, I am not going home with anyone.

We get through the line and into the club and the whole

time I'm thinking, a few drinks, a flirt here and there, and then I'm going home.

No screwing whatsoever.

And then I see *him*.

Chapter 2

Zane

I down the third shot of whiskey and relish the burn. It feels good to unwind after a long, hard day of work. Not that I didn't love it. I slam the glass down and lean back, cracking my neck.

I had a great day at the shop. Time flew by, and I loved every minute of it. I only had one client all day, but he was so fucking grateful and happy for the portrait piece I gave him. I used to love the challenge of tattooing portraits, but it got old real quick. It's so draining. Not physically though, but emotionally.

When someone comes in to get a portrait tattooed, more times than not it's because they lost someone close to them. They cry when they come in, and then I have to hear all about it. I don't mind being a shoulder to cry on, but damn. Fucking sucks.

Some days I feel more like a therapist than a tattoo artist.

If it's not a person who's passed away, it's their boyfriend or girlfriend.

A few times I've even turned down requests. Yeah, I lose out on money when that happens, but I'm not going to tattoo a portrait of some chick's ex on her. Not gonna happen. Once a girl came in, only eighteen years old, wanting to get a profile of her "soulmate" on her shoulder. I asked her how long they'd been together. One month. Yeah, I'm not fucking doing that.

I know where to draw the line.

Not today though. A proud pop wanted his son on his bicep, and I was fucking thrilled to make it happen.

I smile to myself and wave at Tony, the bartender closest to me, for another beer.

Jackson's sitting next to me enjoying the club atmosphere. This is a normal night for the two of us. Usually we're surrounded by more of the guys, but tonight the club's packed, and they're on the prowl. He's had a cocky grin on his face ever since we got here, and for good reason.

Jackson's a playboy and every chick knows it, yet they fall right into his lap every night. He's got a classically handsome thing going for him, and he knows how to let charm and alcohol convince any woman to spread her legs for him. He's young and stupid, and going to knock up one of these broads one day.

He likes his reputation though. I don't get it. He's had

more than one woman come up and slap him for fucking her in the back room and then leaving to go make out with someone else. He's a fucking asshole. Every time, he just takes the hit and smiles. Like I said. Playboy. Asshole.

I'd prefer it if Needles were sitting next to me, but he had shit to do tonight. So I'm left with Jackson.

He drums his fingers on the bartop and looks at me as he asks, "Hard day?" He's asking 'cause of the shots I'm knocking back, I'm sure. I'm not usually a heavy drinker. And if I'm being honest with myself, these shots aren't because of the pride I have from today's work. But I'd rather not think about the shit that's eating at me. It's not like I can change it.

Today's been a hard day, but not because of work. And no one here needs to know why. I school my expression and decide to focus on all the good shit going on in my life.

"Nah, fucking fabulous." He snorts a laugh like he doesn't believe me. "Not joking. Great day at the shop."

He nods his head as Tony pushes our beers toward us. Cindy, the other bartender, looks pissed that Tony was the one to give us the beers. I'm not sure if she's after Jackson's dick or mine. I couldn't really give two shits if she's after me though. I just wanna drink and be distracted enough to forget. I'm not interested in women tonight. I make a mental note to avoid her for the rest of the night.

If it's Jackson she's after, she can have him. She knows what she's getting into.

Jackson turns his back to the bar and faces the dance floor. The lights are dim, but the strobe and spotlights in the center of the room are enough to see all the women shaking their asses and putting on a show.

He stretches out and takes in the view. He does this shit all the time. Like it's a fucking buffet. He does get all the pussy he wants, but he could at least be modest about it. Shit, I'm way better looking than that motherfucker, and even I don't brag about tail as much as him. Being a playboy isn't my thing though. Maybe I'm just pickier.

"Which one tonight?" he says with his typical cocky grin.

The bass drowns out the sounds of all the chatter and clinking of the glasses behind the bar.

And that's when I see her. She's fucking stunning.

I notice the pretty little blonde the moment she walks in. She's curvy in all the right ways, and just my type.

I wasn't in the mood for a lay tonight, but seeing that gorgeous body, fuck yeah I am now. *She* could be the distraction I need. I know her body can take a punishing fuck. Thick thighs, and an even thicker ass. Her hips sway a little as she walks.

I find myself mesmerized as she takes a seat at the far end of the bar. I watch her for a minute, waiting for her to look my way. She looks everywhere but at me, and it's starting to piss me off.

My brow furrows, hating that I can't get this broad's

attention.

She's fucking gorgeous and I already know I want her. Tonight. In my bed. I'm definitely taking this sweet little thing home with me. I watch as her clutch slips off the bar top and she lets out a little yelp, nervously looking around to see if anyone noticed.

A short brunette sitting next to her says something I can't hear, and then belts out a loud laugh and nearly twirls in her seat like the barstool is gonna spin for her.

I hadn't noticed her friend before; too busy eyeing up that ass. My girl looks embarrassed by her friend but smiles anyway, shaking her head.

I can see the two of them being friends. A sassy over-the-top chick with a trendy bob and a more traditional beauty who'd keep her in line. I bet between the two of 'em, the brunette will be the first on the dance floor. I can only hope her friend lets loose and I can squeeze in to take her spot on the barstool.

Her gorgeous green eyes finally catch mine but she's quick to look away with an innocent blush. I let a smirk kick up the corner of my lips. She's fucking cute. And she's got a pouty mouth and a heart-shaped face that add to the innocent look. I'd love to see those lips wrapped around my cock.

I stifle a groan as my dick hardens in my pants at that last thought. It's been a while, a long while since I buried myself in some hot pussy.

She looks like a good girl though, and I don't think it's an act. That could be a problem. Or maybe it could add to the fun.

I've seen girls come in here acting all cute and innocent, but what they really want is some thick gangster cock. Just so they can say they got dirty with a bad boy. A few shots and they're taking off their tops, letting anyone in here play with their tits.

I take another look at my sexy-as-fuck blonde and she's still a little stiff as she orders a drink. Right now I wish Tony would let Cindy take over that end of the bar. He's quick to get their orders and adds a little flourish to the pour of citrus vodka before adding some tonic or some shit to it. A girly drink. Yeah, she's definitely a good girl.

Her friend orders a Long Island Iced Tea, and I snort. Of course she would. I clench my teeth. That drink could put a wrench in my plans. I'm not sure I want her friend getting wasted. I need Blondie coming home with me, not babysitting her reckless friend.

Blondie cocks her head and her friend holds up one finger. I grin. Good. Well that solves that problem.

The two of them keep chatting, but it's mostly her friend doing the talking while Blondie just shakes her head and smiles. I can't hear a damn thing they're saying over the music.

I wish I could. I'm trying to think of how to cut in and lay on the charm. But I don't know shit about this broad.

My girl looks like she doesn't belong here. And she doesn't. Neither of them do. This is where the Koranav hangout. Everyone knows it in this town. The women in here are dancing to catch our attention. The men are Koranavs or prospects, or maybe associates. They're all men who are in on the business. Everyone knows what this place really is. Cops too, but they can't prove a damn thing.

Not that it matters. This is just where we hang out and relax, not do business. To be honest, I still don't feel like I fit in here. Not unless Needles is with me, or Nikolai.

I may be under the boss's thumb, but I don't like associating with most of these pricks. I look to my right. Like Jackson. I could do without this asshole. Still, it's nice to get a drink. And in this town, this is *the* place to go to unwind.

Plus it's expected of me. If I didn't show up... well, that's not a good look.

This sweet little thing obviously doesn't know shit. And it doesn't look like her friend does either. I want it to be true 'cause that makes it all the more challenging, and it means she doesn't already have an opinion of who I am and what I do.

Blondie twists in her seat to reach down from her spot on the stool. The sight of her bending over to pick up her clutch makes my dick jump in my pants. Her long blonde hair sways gently as she sits upright and finally relaxes a bit.

I catch her peeking up at me through her thick lashes, but I keep my gaze focused on the TV at the back of the bar. I watch from the corner of my eyes as she takes a sip of her drink and a small smile slips into place. She sets the glass down carefully on the napkin and takes another covert look around.

The guys have eyes on her even though she doesn't know it. Plenty of cops have come in here. We don't do business here for that reason. It'd be fucking stupid to.

It's obvious to me she's not undercover, but the easiest way to tell if a woman is a cop is to try to fuck 'em. Jackson gets up from his seat next to me and licks his lips. His eyes are steady on the two of them.

That's not gonna fucking happen. Not her, and not her friend. He'd blow this for me for sure.

I strong-arm him, stopping him from getting all the way up and his ass falls back onto the stool. A few people look up interestedly, including Blondie, but I don't give a fuck. I shake my head with a grin, and the fucker actually pouts like I just took away his puppy.

She's mine, and he's not ruining this for me.

He looks me in the eyes and grudgingly gives in. "Fine, she's all yours."

I may not be high in the ranks. Shit they may not even think I really belong here, but I can sure as fuck call dibs on whoever I want. Simply because I'm a tough motherfucker, and everyone in here knows I could take them if I wanted. Shit, Vlad wanted me as a muscle man in the mob. Took a lot of guts for me to tell him it wasn't going to happen. I wanted my shop and my art more than anything else. I thought it was going to be a showdown. Thank fuck for Nikolai.

Either way, I'm all hard muscle and every fucker in here

knows not to mess with me. A few had to learn the hard way. A few others picked fights with me just to see if they'd win. I'd be lying if I said I wasn't a bit cocky about going undefeated. Either way, Jackson has a reputation for fucking. Mine is for fighting.

If I want something, I'm gonna get it and no one's stupid enough to get in my way. Of course if it was Vlad or Nikolai, it'd be a different story. The boss and the underboss are two people I don't fuck with.

But they aren't here tonight, and no one's gonna stop me from pulling that dress up and feasting on that delicious pussy I know is between those thick thighs.

I down my beer and get up, ready to find out how sweet and innocent Blondie really is.

Chapter 3

Madeline

Trouble.

That's the only word I can think of when I lay eyes on the stranger dressed all in black. Tall, dark-haired and incredibly handsome, the dude literally takes my breath away. At the other end of the bar with one other guy and throwing back shots of what I think is whiskey, he's sitting there, staring at me with an intensity that makes me shiver all the way from across the room.

I can't get over how handsome this guy is, tattoos and all. Seriously, I'm not one for tattoos, but this guy is so sexy that his ink only adds to his appeal.

I stare back, challenging him to look away. He doesn't,

and I'm almost spellbound by the way he continues to look at me. His gaze is so intense that I swear that my ovaries are doing the hokey-pokey.

But why is he staring at just me?

I know I'm not ugly, but there's a sea of beautiful women on the dance floor who are probably more than willing go home with this guy and ride him like a mechanical bull.

Who says he's looking at me because he wants to take me home and have sex? I wonder, even though I know that's what most men in the club are here for. *He might just think I look good.*

I'm comforted by the thought and feel a surge of confidence at being admired, but the look in the handsome man's eyes says otherwise. It seems to say, 'You're mine, and there's nothing you can do about it.'

I'm suddenly irritated by this. This is a guy, I feel, who's used to getting his way with women.

Well, he won't have his way with me, I vow. *I don't care how hot he is.*

I'm about to turn my nose up, you know, to give him the proverbial snub, when the guy sitting next to him jumps up. I hadn't noticed him until this moment, but he's a hot piece of ass himself, and I wouldn't mind it if he came over to say hi. But oh no, Mr. Sexier's ass isn't having it. He jumps up right after him and practically strong-arms the poor guy back down into his seat. The two exchange words before Mr. Sexier turns his intense gaze back on me. My heart thumps in my chest.

Oh no he didn't.

"Holy shit!" Katie exclaims over the heavy thumping bass of the music and gawks. Just a second ago she'd been laughing with some annoying douche who'd bought her a mixed drink, but apparently she has her eyes on the two of them, too. "Did you just see that? Dude just made that kid sit down like he was in time out."

My mouth open and suddenly dry, I'm unable to respond because Mr. Sexier begins moving through the sea of undulating bodies toward our end of the bar. Even the way he moves is sexy, gliding forward with incredible swagger.

"I gotta go," I squeak suddenly, ready to make a run for it. There's no way I'm sticking around to be accosted by Satan himself.

"Oh no you don't, missy," Katie growls, clamping an arm down on my wrist and holding me in place. "You're going to sit right here until Mr. Tall Bottle of Champagne gets to meet you."

"Let me go," I hiss, watching the man, who's almost halfway to us. I can't believe Katie is doing this to me. I'm totally petrified. "I don't wanna talk to that guy."

Katie scowls at me in disbelief. "You're crazy. Do you see how hot he is?" She stares right at him, and I wanna hide. She's making it so obvious!

"That's the very reason I'm trying to get away. Now let go!" I try to pry her fingers off, but Katie is a stubborn bitch.

"No," Katie refuses. "You're going to give this guy a

chance. Live a little."

Bitch.

I tug sharply, trying to disengage from Katie's grip and run for safety, but she suddenly appears to have the super strength of Wonder Woman and I'm kept in place. I'm about to summon everything I've got to shove Katie off her barstool, but too late. Trouble has arrived.

"Mind if I have a seat?" asks a deep, sexy voice that sends goosebumps up along my arm. I almost close my eyes as my pussy clenches with need.

I turn to look up into the bluest eyes I've ever seen, and my breath catches in my throat. Now that he's up close, I can see he's even more handsome than he looked from across the bar, if that's even possible. His features are perfectly chiseled, with a strong jawline, sharp cheekbones and a cleft in his chin. The way his dark hair hangs down just above his eyes makes him look all the more enigmatic.

I can see the tattoo on his arm clearly now. It's a serpent, and it's a beautiful piece of art. It wraps around his arm in a tight coil. The rest of the sleeve is jam-packed with a combination of scrolls and intricate designs, with layers of colors that blend seamlessly. I find my eyes focusing on all the detail and wondering how long it took. Hours, no, days. And holy hell, it must've hurt.

Katie turns in her seat and smiles up at the stranger, acting as if she hasn't just held me hostage. "Not at all, Mr....?"

"Zane," the handsome man supplies.

Fuck. Even his name is sexy. There's no way I'm going to survive this. This is what I get for spending so much time away from men. The first one that gives me any attention is knocking me flat on my ass.

Katie beams and offers her hand. "Nice to meet you, Zane. I'm Katie, and this is my friend Madeline."

I lean over and whisper in Katie's ear, "I am SO going to kill you for this."

Zane quickly shakes Katie's hand and then offers me his. I stare at it for a moment like it's a snake before taking it. The minute our hands touch, I feel a jolt of electricity go up my arm. Seriously, it's like a thousand volts just shot through my body and I swear my hair must be sticking up like I just stuck my finger in a power outlet. I wanna pull away, but I can't. I'm paralyzed.

"Nice to meet you, Madeline," Zane says in that deep, throaty voice of his, shaking my hand, unaware that his touch is doing some serious things to my body. After a moment, he lets go of my hand and I feel a twinge of disappointment.

"Nice to meet you, too," I manage, but I'm barely audible over the music and I'm sure Zane doesn't hear me. He doesn't seem to care though, and his eyes continue to burn into me.

Katie suddenly jumps off her stool. "I was just telling Maddy here that I needed to take a tinkle." She motions at the packed bar. "You can have my seat until I get back." Oh.

My. God. She did not just say tinkle. Kill me now.

Before I can object, Katie takes off like a speed demon, leaving me all alone with Zane.

Katie, you are dead, I send telepathically, wishing bad luck on my best friend for her treachery.

Zane nods at Katie's seat. "You mind?" I catch a whiff of alcohol on his breath. Whiskey. I don't drink whiskey. Personally, I hate it. But the faint smell of it on his breath combined with his unique, masculine smell makes me want to lean into him.

Do you even have to ask?

I'm actually kind of surprised by Zane's manners, considering that he looks like a fellow who takes what he wants without asking.

Not trusting myself to speak, I shake my head. Zane grins and sits down next to me. Being this close to him, I feel my body temperature rise. I almost feel like I need a fan.

Not noticing my discomfort, Zane signals the bartender, but the man who poured my earlier drink nods to the female bartender. She's a slim brunette with big tits. She's in the middle of serving some guy a drink, but I swear she puts on speed boots to get over to us.

"What will it be, honey?" she rasps breathlessly, looking like she's ready to bend over right then and there and let Zane fuck her in front of the entire crowd. Suddenly I'm wishing the other bartender were here, and not this bimbo.

I start to look away to give them some fucking privacy, but Zane doesn't pay her an ounce of attention and replies, "A cosmo for my lady friend here."

What the hell? I wonder. *Is he a mind reader, too?*

"Nothing for you, *Zane*?" she asks, putting emphasis on his name. I'm reading her loud and clear, but if Zane is, he isn't showing it.

"Nah," he says, putting a hand on my barstool, a little too close to my ass. "Just my girl's drink." *My girl's?* I feel a blush rise up my chest and into my cheeks. I have to admit, being called his girl feels nice. But I'm quick to push those emotions down.

The bartender looks at me for a second with disdain, and then she looks back at Zane and winks. "One cosmo, coming right up." She sashays off to the mixer, swinging her hips with every step.

I decide to ignore both his hand and claim on me and instead I gape at Zane with shock when she's gone. "How the hell did you know I liked cosmos?"

Zane grins, a boyish grin that makes my inner voice scream at me to run away now before it's too late. "I'm good at reading women." His eyes seem to say, 'That's not the only thing I'm good at, either.' And I believe it.

"Can you read my horoscope, too?" I ask playfully. *You know, the one that says that if I don't get away from you now, I'm in serious trouble?*

"Huh?" he asks and I almost laugh.

Instead I smile and toy with the empty glass in front of me, running my fingers down the stem and leaning into the bar. I shake my head and say, "Nothing."

The brunette's back in a flash with my drink. "Anything else, handsome?" She's trying hard to get Zane's attention, practically sticking her tits in his face. But he only has eyes for me.

"Nah, that's all." He tries to give her a tip, but she pushes it away.

"It's on the house," she purrs as another patron calls for her service. She leaves with a wink, saying, "If you need anything else, just holler. It's always my pleasure to please."

I'm not absolutely certain, but I'm pretty sure Miss Minx was letting Zane know that she's down to fuck whenever he's ready.

"Do you get that all the time?" I have to ask, even though I already know the answer. He's fucking hot. Of course he does.

Zane shrugs as if it's no big deal. "I'm used to it." He stares at me. "You're not from around here, are you?"

Yep. He's a mind reader.

Shaking my head, I take a sip of my cosmo. I'm impressed. It's actually really good. I half-wonder if she spit in it though, just to spite me. "No, actually. Katie and I are new in town. We move into our new place tomorrow."

Zane looks very interested. "Oh yeah? Where at?"

Alarm bells go off in my head. *Don't tell him where.* I don't know why I don't want to tell Zane where I'll be living. It's not like he would stalk me considering he can have any woman he wants.

"1212 Candyland Road," I lie. And the first cosmo must be hitting me, because that is a horrible street name to think up. This town isn't that big. He's gonna know.

Zane makes a face. "Candyland Road? I've lived here all my life and never heard of that street."

I gesture vaguely and take another sip. "It's near the edge of town."

"Oh, okay." From his demeanor, I can tell Zane knows I'm bullshitting, but he doesn't press the issue. He gives me a grin and leans forward, looking like my lie was more amusing than anything else.

"Aren't you going to order yourself a drink?" I ask. I really don't wanna get wasted while he's sober. I'm actually surprised he's not showing any signs of being tipsy with those shots he downed.

"Nah. I think I've had one too many shots of whiskey."

"I saw." I smile playfully. "How about something a little lighter, then? Like my cosmo?" It's not in my nature to share a drink, but the thought of this man taking a sip from this girly glass makes me smile. Shit, maybe I'm already a little tipsier than I thought.

"Nah. Not my style. Besides, cosmos are pussy drinks."

I know I should be turned off by his crude words and the diss on my drink, but the way he says "pussy" summons up the image of him down in between my legs and his powerful jaws clamped down on my muff.

Jesus, I haven't even known him more than five minutes and I'm already thinking dirty thoughts. Get a hold of yourself, Maddy!

"Hey, they're not that bad," I protest, hoping he's not clued in to the dirty image flashing through my mind. My nipples are hard, and my breathing is coming up short though. I clear my throat and take a quick drink. I need to get a grip.

"I'll stick with whiskey, or vodka," he replies as he shakes his head.

"You're missing out," I say as I take another sip of my drink.

"Doubt it. I only like sweet things when I'm eating them." The way he looks at me drives home his pun.

I nearly spit out my drink into his lap. Holy crap. Did the bastard know I was just thinking about him between my legs? I try hard not to let on that I'm picking up what he's throwing down, but judging by the smirk on his face, he knows exactly what I'm thinking. Cocky bastard.

"So what brings you two to this shithole town?" Zane asks, looking as if he's trying not to laugh at my reaction. "Wait, let me guess. You're both going to the state university?"

I gulp, trying to keep my mind clear of that image of him eating me out. "Yeah."

He grins. "I knew it."

"What about you? Do you go to college there, too?"

A dark shadow passes over Zane's face and I feel like I've

hit a nerve. "No," he says flatly after a second. That heat flowing through my body chills some. He obviously didn't like that question. Shit, I'm not buzzed enough not to realize his displeasure. It was just an innocent question though. I retreat to my drink.

The beats of the music fills the silence that ensues, and I wonder if Zane's decided I'm not worth his trouble. I figure the conversations he has with the women in places like these usually revolve around how soon can he take them home to his bed, not getting to know you type stuff.

"So, what do you do?" I dare ask when the silence between us stretches on for more than thirty seconds.

Zane seems to perk up at the question. "I'm a tattoo artist," he says proudly.

"Really?" Tattoos really aren't my thing, but I have respect for people with artistic talent. "That's pretty cool. I've never known a real artist before." I turn in my seat to face him. I really like that he has a job that's... different.

"Yeah. I own my own shop, Inked Envy on Second Street." He points at the serpent tattoo on his arm. "I gave myself this one."

I gawk. The whole thing is so beautiful. "You did this yourself?"

He nods. That's impressive. I know next to nothing about tattoos, but I know that had to be hard.

"How?" I can't even imagine how long that took. I look at

his right arm and see there's no tattoos on that arm.

"I'm good at what I do," he says matter-of-factly, without a trace of bragging in his voice.

"Wow." Unconsciously, I reach out to touch his arm, feeling along the length of the tattoo. His muscles bulge underneath my touch, and once again, sparks seem to pop off his skin.

"Your hands feel so soft," Zane says, grabbing hold of my wrist and pulling me in close. He runs his finger up along my arm, shooting off more sparks. "I could fix you up, free of charge. Would you like that?" It takes a moment for me to realize he's asking about a tattoo.

I have an immediate urge to say yes, but I don't, and I stare at him, trembling in his grasp. In that moment, I'm more afraid than I've ever been in my life.

I feel like he has absolute power over me. His question could have been, "Will you come home and have sex with me?" and I would have said yes.

That's it. I have to get away.

"Sorry, gotta go!" Not giving him a chance to respond, I jerk out of his grasp and quickly disappear into the crowd of people grinding on the dance floor. I look around for Katie, but don't see her beneath all the flashing lights. Moving as fast as I can, I make my way into the club's hallway and stop to rest against the wall.

I breathe in and out, trying to get a hold of myself, my legs shaking. All I can think about is how close I came to losing control, and Zane had only asked if I wanted him to give me a tattoo!

"Where do you think you're going, sweet thing?" asks a deep voice that makes my knees weak.

Oh no.

I try to make a run for it, but suddenly I'm sandwiched between the wall and a rock-hard body.

Fuck.

"Did I say you could leave?" Zane growls in my face. His voice is soft and sexy, not meant to be a threat, only a dare to stay. The smell of whiskey is even stronger on his breath at this distance. Instead of disgusting me, it only makes me more turned on. His hot breath makes my nipples pebble. My core is soaked and my pussy is clenching around nothing. This isn't good. I fucking *want* him. Every inch of my body craves him.

"Y-y-you're not my daddy," I stammer, ignoring every instinct in me.

"No. I'm not." Zane gives me a cocky grin, moving in closer. "But I can be... if you want."

I'm almost on fire. My dress seems to be rising up my thighs, practically inviting Zane in. "What are you talking about?" I have to close my eyes and will the naughty images away.

"I think you know," he whispers in my ear.

I do know. And it would be so easy to give in, so easy to just melt in his arms. And he *wants* me. He *chased* me. That has to mean something.

"You know you want it." He says it as if his words are a dare.

He's right. I do want it. So fucking badly. My body is burning. Every inch of me wants him inside of me, even right here in this hallway. I don't care who sees.

Zane inches in closer as if coming in for a kiss. If his lips touch mine, I know it's all over.

I can't do this!

"Get the fuck off me!" I yell out as the thought of him sliding my dress up and fucking me against the wall becomes a very real possibility.

At the last possible second, I summon every ounce of self-control I can muster and shove Zane away from me. Then I take off like a jackrabbit down the hall, and out the club, not daring to look back.

Chapter 4

Zane

I watch Maddy's back as she practically runs from me. Her hands grip the hem of her dress as she pulls it farther down her thighs. She's speeding off like I just told her I was a hitman and she's on my list.

What the fuck?

I stand dumbfounded in a lust-filled haze. She's leaving? It takes a moment and the sounds of the club filling my ears to realize she's really gone. I was two seconds away from crashing my lips against hers and inching her dress up to give her the release she needs. Well maybe not here, where anyone could watch, unless she'd be into that.

She pushed me away. What the fuck did I do? I replay

everything in my head, but I don't know where I crossed the line.

She had to know I'd follow her out here. Shit, I know she didn't think I'd let her get away that easy.

And she was loving it. I know she wants me. Or wanted me. Fuck!

By the time I think about chasing her and head out to the exit, she's nowhere in sight.

I push past the crowd and jog my way to the front. She's not here. I check every dark corner, but Maddy's fucking gone.

I search the dance floor and find her friend. Fuck me, but I can't remember her name for the life of me. Did she even tell me?

She's dancing with a group of women, having a blast and not paying attention to anything.

I have to grab her arm to get her attention.

She whips around like she's gonna bitchslap me until she recognizes me. Her eyes dart around me and she looks confused. Shit, that's not a good sign. I was hoping Maddy went to her before going wherever it is she went.

I scream over the music, "I lost your friend!"

"Fuck!" she yells out and starts pushing past me and everyone else, making a beeline for the door.

I follow her outside. Shit, did I really chase her off to the point where she felt like she had to leave?

I turn to look at her friend who's now got her cell phone to her ear. She's got one finger shoved into the opposite ear to drown out the sound of all the people still waiting in line. The bouncer's watching us, but I give him a quick nod.

"You good?" he asks with his brows raised. I give him a short nod. I'm not really good though. This fucking sucks. And I feel like shit for pushing her away like that.

"Goddamn it," her friend mutters after looking down the sidewalk and shoving her phone into her clutch.

She makes a move to go back inside.

"Did she leave?" I ask her.

She shrugs her shoulders and says, "Sorry." She gives me a sad look and a tight smile before making a move to open the door. Fuck.

I get it for her, opening it wide enough, but I don't go in.

"You think you could give me Maddy's number?" I ask her with a little embarrassment. I don't think I've ever asked for a chick's number before. And definitely not from her friend. She looks like she's considering it, but then she scrunches her nose and shakes her head.

"I'm sorry." She really does look apologetic. "I'll bring her ass back here though." She nods her head confidently.

"That's alright." I watch her go in as my hope of seeing Maddy again dwindles.

I stand outside the club feeling the crisp cold air of the night against my skin. The bass of the music beats in my ears and it pisses me off.

Anger replaces confusion. Not at Maddy, but at myself.

I knew she was too much of a good girl. I needed to play it smooth and slow, and instead I went for the kill too fast and freaked her out.

But damn, I couldn't help myself. Feeling her body against mine... I stifle my groan.

I just had my hands all over that lush ass. I could practically feel how tight that hot pussy was gonna be cumming all over my dick. Speaking of my dick, the damn thing is currently hard as fucking steel in my jeans.

What the fuck did I do? She was all over me. She wanted me just as much as I wanted her. She felt so good with her curvy body pushed against mine. And she would've felt even better impaled on my dick. She was so fucking responsive, and I can only imagine what she'd be like under me.

I take another look around the crowd and then back down the sidewalk to the left and the right. She's not there. Fuck! I pushed too hard, too fast.

I run my hands through my hair and clear my throat.

Well, shit. That fucking sucks. I close my eyes and remember the soft, sweet sounds of her moans. My dick jumps in my pants and I have to turn and head back inside.

I need a drink.

I make it halfway there when a hot platinum blonde with a tight ass and perky tits stops in front of me.

"Hey handsome, I was looking to get out of here." Her perfect white teeth bite down slightly on her bottom lip, drawing my eyes to her mouth. Vixen is the first term that comes to mind as I take her in.

"I could use a ride," she whispers in a low, sultry voice.

Her lips are almost the same shade of red as her dress, and I have to admit that any other night with my dick this hard, I'd take her up on her offer, but not tonight. Not after Maddy.

"Not tonight." I give her a tight smile and move to walk past her. Her eyes narrow and she looks like she's gonna yell at me for some perceived insult, but then she remembers where she is.

"Fine, asshole," she grumbles as she pushes past me with her fake tits brushing my forearm.

I watch her walk off sashaying her ass and going right for another Koranav member. Yeah, she just wants to get fucked by a mobster. Doesn't matter who. I grit my teeth, feeling more agitated than anything else.

As I head to the back, all the thoughts I've been avoiding start coming to the surface. Fuck, I was feeling so damn good tonight.

Maddy took that away. She was a beautiful distraction. But she fucking took off, and with every step I take I want more and more just to drown myself in a bottle to forget this shit. She could've distracted me tonight. She could've taken that pain away, even if it was just for the night.

I walk back to the bar and my stool is taken by some redhead who's got her legs spread and wrapped around Jackson's thighs. His tongue is down her throat and his hands are up her dress. Usually I don't give a shit, but tonight it pisses me off.

"Wanna buy me a drink?" I turn my head to the left as I rest my hands on the bar and see a second redhead standing there. She's sweet and cute, not like the viper in the red dress from a minute ago, but I can't get Maddy out of my head. I give her a tight smile, 'cause it's all I can manage.

"Sure thing." I keep my voice even and casual. A smile lights up the broad's face. She's gonna be real disappointed in a minute.

I yell at Tony, "Her next drink's on me!" and then turn back to her. "Have a good night, sweetheart." I leave cash on the bar and head out, ignoring the protests from the pretty little thing I'm leaving behind.

At least she got a free drink out of it. She'll find someone else. I'm just not in the mood.

I turn on my heels, giving Tony a curt nod when he catches my gaze. He looks like he wants to ask a question, but I'm not one who likes to talk. He should know that by now.

I walk out the back exit where it's less crowded and get in my Audi without a second thought.

Damn, tonight could've been so fucking good.

The drive is an easy one. I live close to work, and play

close to work, too. It makes life easy.

I twist my hands on the leather steering wheel and grip on tighter. I fucking hate today. Not what happened, just the fucking date. It always reminds me of things I'd love to never have to think about again. Every year it seems to get worse.

As if knowing I'm feeling like shit, Nikolai calls. His name and number pop up on my dash and whatever fucking music was playing is replaced by a ringtone. I push the button to answer as the streetlight turns green.

"Nikolai," I keep my answer short, and my voice even. He's the underboss, and in a way the one person who saved me. I hardly talk to him or to the boss, Vlad. But every year he reaches out, without fail. He's the only one who knows how much it affected me.

"I'm sorry, Zane; I forgot." His voice is etched with sincerity, and I believe him. "I went to the club expecting to find you there, but they said you just left."

I trust him alone out of all the Koranavs. He never shows emotion. Never. It's something that makes you appear weak in this line of business. Even Vlad's anger and hot temper make him look like a loose cannon in my eyes. But on this date every year, Nikolai always opens up to me. He's done this ever since it all happened.

"No need to apologize. I'm doing alright." As I say the words, the pain comes down harder on me. I twist my hands on the leather again and glance out the window as I come to another stop. I just wanna get home now.

"I'd believe you if you went home with some pussy, but they said you didn't." He says it with a touch of humor in his voice and it gets a short, rough laugh from me. I run my hand through my hair and stare at the stoplight.

I remember the feel of Maddy's ass in my hands, and my dick starts to harden. Yeah, I'll be fucking fine. As long as I can work and fuck, I'm fan-fucking-tastic. I try to forget Maddy and her soft curves. Fuck. I close my eyes, willing my dick to not get hard for a woman I can't fucking have. I haven't jerked off in years, not when I can get laid whenever I want. I'm sure as shit not doing that tonight.

"Promise you, it's all good," I tell him.

"If you say so." From his tone I can tell he doesn't believe me. I don't blame him. Anyone who was forced to kill his father would be fucked up. Even if his father was an abusive fuck like my old man.

It happened years ago, but fuck me, I can't let it go.

I was only ten or so when I started stepping in front of my mom to take the hits. I couldn't stand the way he hurt her. I tried to protect her. I thought I was doing the right thing. I thought she loved me.

I woke up one morning to him screaming about how "the bitch left." The beatings only got worse after that. Because of course to my father, I was the reason she left. It's hard to imagine it wasn't true. Why else did she leave me with him?

My old man was more than just an abusive drunk though. He was a degenerate gambler, and got into some serious debt with the mob.

Nikolai, Vlad and two soldiers who are probably long dead came for him when I was fourteen. They found him beating the shit out of me, but I was fighting back. I didn't have much weight to me since I'd barely hit puberty, but it didn't stop me from fighting back.

The mob doesn't like witnesses though, even if they are just kids.

Nikolai spoke up for me. Said he'd teach me. Vlad put a gun in my hand and gave me a choice. Kill my father and join them, or die with my father.

It might sound like an easy choice, but it was harder to pull that trigger than I thought it would be. So many nights had passed where I wanted him dead. I swore one day I'd kill him for what he did to my Ma, and what he did daily to me. But when it came time, I almost chose to die with him.

He stared up at me and instead of telling me to do it to save my life, he called me every name in the book and spit on me. Maybe he did it to make it easier for me. But maybe he really did fucking hate me.

I think you always love your parents somewhere deep down inside. Even if they don't love you back. Even if they don't deserve it.

If it wasn't for Nikolai, I never would've survived.

"Yeah, I'm alright. Just wanna crash tonight," I tell him. "I've got an appointment tomorrow I wanna get up earlier for." That's true in a way.

"Good to hear. It's always nice to get lost in your work." I can see him nodding the way he does. I grew up with Nikolai as my only father figure despite the fact he's not even a decade older than me. It wasn't optimal, but at least I had someone.

It sure is fucking nice to get lost in work. He taught me that. I'm not gonna lie, I was a fucking punk kid growing up. I graffitied everything I could. Got in trouble a few times for it. The first time I went to jail wasn't for fighting, it was for tagging an abandoned building.

Nikolai was pissed. He said the mob doesn't need delinquents, and getting in trouble for dumb shit puts a target on my back. So he got me a job at a tattoo parlor. They smuggled drugs out the back of it. I didn't care though. I just wanted to get my art out there. And Nikolai said it'd be good for me. He told me not to fuck up, and to take it seriously.

I got a reputation pretty fast--a damn good one, and the family hooked me up with my own shop. I was eighteen with my own business, and had clients who fucking loved me. The only condition the mob gave me was that they would handle the books, and they were free to use the back for whatever they needed. I signed that day without thinking much on it.

A few weeks in, Garret and Vlad came into my shop and told me they needed me to cover up a tattoo on a body. I wanted to say no, but I knew better. She was a young girl, maybe my own age, and a member of an MC gang. Garret tossed her on my table and said the tattoo that could identify her needed to be covered. Her body was covered with bruises of varying colors, making me wonder how long they'd tortured her. But what was worse was that she was still bleeding. They'd used a knife on her and mutilated her.

I almost threw up looking at the poor girl. Vlad said they'd "had a little too much fun with her." I kept my composure and quickly added a layer of art to the dead girl's tattoo, but I knew then what kind of sick fucks they were, and that I didn't want anything to do with them. But it was too late. I didn't have a choice. The memory sends a wave of sickness through me. I thought then that I'd have to get used to that shit, but it's only happened the one time. Thank fuck. Other than that day, they stay out of my business, and I stay out of theirs.

I hate being under the mob's thumb.

I can't deny that they could have killed me. Nikolai saved my life, and gave me something to be proud of. And I do love my shop and my work.

I wish it was just mine. After all, people come to me for a reason. They want a Zane original. My art on their bodies.

Maddy comes to mind as I think about how I'd love to put my art on her. I start thinking about what I'd go with, but then I push that thought away. It's pointless to think about.

I pull up to my condo, coming to terms with the fact that

I'll probably never see her again. To my left I see a car I don't recognize at the neighbor's place. I'm always aware of that shit. Just in case. You can never be too laidback when you're involved with the mob.

I guess they finally got the place rented out.

It's a cute little car. I'd bet good money a woman drives it. I check out the tags as I lock up my Audi. The locks slam down, and a small beep rings through the night.

Georgia.

Whoever they are, they're a long way from home.

Chapter 5

Madeline

"Watch what you're doing with that!" Katie yells at one of the moving men who's attempting to pick up a heavy ornamental vase from inside the moving truck. It's the day after the disastrous night at the club, and we're busy moving into our new condo. Despite what happened last night, I'm pretty excited about starting a new chapter in my life. "That's a special gift my mom gave me as a graduation present!" she squawks.

"Sorry," apologizes the young guy, who looks barely older than eighteen. He gently picks up the vase and carefully walks off the van, moving as if he's carrying something worth more than gold.

Hands on her hips, Katie growls, "You better be."

"Jesus, Katie," I complain, shaking my head and wiping at the sweat on my brow. It's a sweltering ninety-five degrees outside and I feel like going inside and flopping down on the floor and enjoying the cool AC, but Katie insists I help her oversee the moving.

At least I'm not one of these guys, I think with sympathy. *They're doing all this hard work for less than minimum wage I bet. And to make matters worse, they have Katie making their lives even more miserable.*

To fight the heat, Katie and I are dressed in cutoff shorts and midriff-baring tank tops, but I'm still sweating like a dog.

"You didn't have to be so mean to the kid. He hadn't even picked it up yet."

Katie turns to scowl at me. "Did we, or did we not pay these guys out of our hard-earned student loan checks?"

I snicker at the thought of our student loans being 'hard-earned'. I guess I know what she meant though, since it's not like we won't be paying exorbitant interest rates after college. "Yeah, but that doesn't mean you can just treat them like that"

Cutting me off, Katie turns to watch the young guy make it off the moving truck and onto the sidewalk with the giant vase. "Okay then. I can tell them whatever I want, especially when they're handling things that are dear to me."

"Psycho," I mutter under my breath, giving up.

"Hey!" Katie screams when the guy almost trips stepping over the sidewalk. Luckily, he regains his balance without dropping Katie's precious vase. "Watch it, clumsy!" After the guy makes it into the condo unscathed, Katie turns on me with a murderous glare. "See," she says flatly.

"Why are you being so bitchy today?" I demand.

"Because I have a nasty hangover." About time she admits it.

"Maybe you shouldn't have drunk so much." I don't know why I even bothered responding though. She never listens to me. At least she didn't wake me up at 3 a.m. by puking into the toilet.

"Maybe you shouldn't have run from the club and left me stranded," she says without missing a beat. Fuck, that hits a nerve. I do feel bad about that. But what the fuck was I supposed to do? She wasn't going to leave with me, and I *needed* to get out of there before I did something I'd regret.

I wipe at a trickle of sweat running down the side of my face. "You know what? I'm too hot to deal with your shit today. Can we not do this, please?"

Katie bites her lower lip and says, "Sorry," even though I know she isn't. "Speaking of hot, I can't believe you turned down that Zane guy!"

"I can. The dude was an asshole." I'm not sure why I'm lying to her. Zane hadn't done anything particularly wrong, unless you can call making me want to have sex with him a crime.

Just speaking about him brings up the memory of how hot I felt against his body, and how much I wanted him inside of me. When he pressed up against me, I could feel it. His cock was fucking *huge*. Somehow I get a little hotter thinking about what he could have done to me with a dick that big. I can't help but feel a little regret, but I know it was the right move to leave him there. Wasn't it?

"Who cares? If it was me, I would've fucked him every which way but sideways even if he'd slapped me around and called me his bitch." She thinks for a moment, and her frown morphs into a naughty smile. "In fact, I think I would rather enjoy that."

"Katie!" Thank God my face is already red from the heat so she can't tell how much the idea of him doing that to me turns me on, too.

Katie looks at me with typical feigned innocence. "Wha? That guy was the hottest guy I've seen in a long time. I would've killed to have him lusting after me like he was after you."

"He wasn't lusting after me," I argue. "He just wanted to buy me a drink."

"He wasn't? Remember how he shoved that other hot guy down in his seat just to get to you?" Fuck, that *was* hot.

"Nope." The word comes out easy as I shake my head.

"Liar. You said he had you up against the wall in the hallway, ready to bang your brains out."

The image of his lips being inches away from mine flashes in front of my eyes and I try hard to push it away. I wish Katie would stop going on about Zane. Thinking about him just makes my temperature rise, and it's already hot as hell.

"What does it matter now anyway? I'll never see him again."

Which is a good thing, I think to myself. *He was nothing but trouble.*

Katie shakes her head at me in sympathy. "You just don't get it, do you? You're so scared to live a little just because of what happened between you and Zach that you're missing out on the simple pleasures in life."

"How is going home with a total stranger and getting screwed by him 'missing out'?" I demand. "If anything, it cheapens me."

"Are you kidding me? That guy was hot as fuck, with a big ass dick to match."

"How do you know he had a big dick?" Despite my question, I agree with Katie. When Zane was pressed up against me, I felt his hard bulge. And if the size of it was an indication of anything, he was hung like a horse.

"Did you see the size of his nose?" she says with a wink.

I roll my eyes. "You're impossible.

"And you need to get laid. Preferably last night. Hey!" Katie yells at the other mover. "Don't carry that like that!"

Katie begins badgering this guy about how to properly carry a box of her precious items of God knows what, even going as far to follow him into the condo, leaving me alone in the hot sun.

I'm about to follow her in when I see a box with my name on it on the back of the truck. If memory serves me correct, it's filled with a bunch of personal hygiene products that I don't want anyone to see. I'll take my tampons in myself, thank you very much.

"I'll just get that, and then I'm staying in the cool air until they're done," I mutter to myself. "I don't care how much Katie bitches and whines at me."

I jump onto the truck and grab the box. It's heavy as hell, but I make it off the truck before I have to set the box down and take a breather.

"Need help with that, peaches?" asks a deep, familiar voice.
Oh my fucking God.

I look up into that cocky grin and those beautiful blue eyes. Instantly, images of last night are back in my mind and I'm filled with burning desire. Dressed only in a pair of blue jeans that are ripped at the knees, Zane is standing in front of me with his shirt off.

I can only marvel at his incredible body. Seriously, his abs looked like they were etched by a grandmaster mason, chiseled to perfection. To make matters worse, a sheen of sweat covers his entire torso, and droplets of sweat are running down the hardened lines of his stomach muscles. I have to fight an extreme urge to want to bend over and lick it off.

If I thought I was burning up before, now I'm in the fiery pits of hell.

"What are you doing here?" I croak with disbelief, trying to keep my eyes level with his face and not that washboard stomach of his.

Zane's grin grows wider and his eyes seem to assess my body, making me feel even hotter. He's pleased that he's shocked me. "I live right there," he says, nodding to the condo that's directly next to mine.

I gape with shock. Seriously, I'm fucking floored. What are the odds? What are the odds that I meet this guy at the bar and run away from him, only to find out that he lives right next door to me?

One in a hundred billion zillion, I think to myself. Fuck! I can't run away from him now.

"You're shitting me."

Zane chuckles. Fuck. Even his laugh is sexy. "Nah. Actually, I was surprised myself when I saw you guys out here. I was like, no way. Apparently fate's decided to bring us back together again." The way he looks at me conjures up the memory of running from his sexy touch. His eyes are telling me I've committed a crime, and he won't let me get away with it.

"Then fate must be fucked up in the head."

Zane throws back his head and laughs again. "You're funny, I'll give you that."

There's nothing funny about this situation. I ran away last night because I knew Zane was nothing but trouble, and now fate's put him right next door.

Almost as if to torment me.

"And sexy," he growls throatily, his eyes roaming all over

my body.

I suddenly remember what I'm wearing, daisy dukes that hug my ass cheeks and a cropped tank top that bares my midriff, and I blush furiously under Zane's appreciative stare.

God, he makes me feel so sexy. Wanted.

"Yeah, somehow fate changed the name of my street to Candyland Road without even telling me."

My cheeks heat with embarrassment. "It's alright peaches," he winks at me.

Right then, Katie comes back out of our condo with one of the moving guys in tow. She stops and stares when she sees Zane, her jaw dropping. After composing herself, she walks over.

"Well, well, well. Look at what we have here," she says with a huge smile plastered on her face.

"Hey," Zane greets her politely.

Katie encircles her arm around Zane's sculpted waistline and looks up at him admiringly. "Sup, hot stuff?"

I roll my eyes at Katie's silliness.

Zane chuckles. "Not much."

"Can you believe he lives right next door?" I demand. For some reason the sight of Katie's arms around Zane is irritating me, though I don't know why. It's not like we're an item. Or like Katie would ever go after a guy I liked. My brow furrows at the thought. *Do* I like him? I only kissed him. It wasn't anything. It's fine. Whatever.

"Nope. Can you believe these abs, though?" she marvels, actually running her hands along Zane's muscular lines that are slick with sweat.

"Get your hands off him!" I snap with so much venom it causes Katie to jump away from Zane.

"Damn, Maddy, I didn't realize he was your property." I bite down on the inside of my cheek and stare at the house.

She's right. I don't know what's come over me. I ran away from Zane like he was the devil last night, and here I am getting pissed because Katie's admiring his perfect body?

"I'm sorry," I apologize to Zane quickly, my cheeks burning from embarrassment. "I don't know what came over me."

Zane has an amused smirk on his face. He doesn't look bothered by my outburst in the least. In fact, I think he liked it. "It's cool."

"And you were calling me bitchy earlier," Katie complains.

"Well you were," I point out.

"Says the one who just screamed at me for touching our hot new neighbor." She raises her voice on the last words and gives him a wink.

I ignore how much I hate that I feel jealous. "I didn't scream."

"You didn't? I think they heard you on the other side of town."

I roll my eyes with exasperation and turn to Zane. "Do you see what I have to deal with?"

Zane chuckles. "I think it's cute."

Katie sticks her tongue out at me. "See Maddy, even Zane takes my side."

"Hey," Zane protests. "Don't put me in the middle of this."

"You sure about that? The three of us would make a good sandwich."

I blush. "Katie!" Jesus. She's so embarrassing. I know she's joking, but he might not!

"Wha?"

I shake my head. "Nevermind." I cross my arms and lean back against the van.

Katie badgers him with question after question about the area and I watch them interact, only half-listening to what he's saying. He keeps looking back at me when he answers, even though I'm not the one asking. And as much as Katie loves pissing me off, she's at least keeping her hands to herself. With every move he makes, his muscles ripple and glisten in the sun. It's not fair. Fate really is a bitch.

"So, you going to help us out then?" Katie asks him. It's only when he answers he's more than happy to oblige that I realize he's staying to help the movers. Which means he'll be in our house.

"I gotta go inside," I bite out and push off the van.

"You alright?" Zane asks.

I fan myself and walk backward. "Just need to cool off."

"You're telling me," Katie says with a smirk. I roll my eyes and nearly fall flat on my face as I try to turn around and walk normally. Fuck. I am not looking back. I refuse to check to see if he saw me.

Despite saying I was going to go inside and enjoy the A/C, I watch Zane at work, admiring his glistening muscles and washboard abs until they're done. Which happens all too quickly. I fucking hated packing, but I'd go out and buy all of Ikea if I could right now. I wish I had some new furniture I could ask him to assemble for me, giving me an excuse to check him out some more.

I grab a case of water from the kitchen and set it on the table for the guys. It's the least we can do.

It looks like Katie has set her sights on a new man and is chatting with one of the movers as the guys walk out.

I give them a wave and yell after them, "Thanks again!"

My heart beats faster as Zane, at the very end of the line, closes the door, rather than walking through it.

Oh, fuck.

I can't run now.

I grab a bottle of water and walk to the kitchen to start unpacking, completely ignoring the fact that he followed me in here. This is bad. I'm hot and sweaty and worked up. My lungs aren't even working right.

I stand near the fridge and consider bending down to open the closest box, but I know I need to say something. I look up and I'm trying desperately not to stare at him and his sweaty, hot body. Trying desperately not to think naughty thoughts. Trying, and failing miserably.

He's leaning against the sink, looking at me with hunger in his eyes.

"Would you like a drink?" I offer the bottle, holding it out to him. He has to know I'm so horny I can't think straight, and I can't stand being this close to him right now.

"No. I'm good." He pushes off the sink and takes a step forward. I'd take a step back, but the wall is right there.

"Why are you here?" I ask him.

"You know why." I do, but I lie.

"No, I don't."

He walks over and pushes me up against the wall, cornering me. His hot, sweaty body is inches away from mine. My chest feels tight.

A feeling of déjà vu sweeps through me.

"You owe me."

His eyes seem to say, 'You won't be escaping this time.' His hand grabs my hip. Not a single part of me even thinks about pushing him away.

"Owe you what?" I ask in a hushed voice.

"This."

He kisses me, and my body comes alive with electricity. Everywhere he touches me sends sparks of desire straight to my core. I groan and lean into him. He can have me, right here. Right now.

No, Maddy! You have to stop!

I don't know how I do it, but I summon the will to shove him away. "Get out!" I gasp, stabbing a finger at the door. I'm shaking all over. Just a few seconds more and I would have been ready to have this man's babies.

Frustration flashes across Zane's eyes, but it's gone in an instant. "If that's what you want," he says.

It's not what I want. I want him to take me right there and fuck my brains out. Zane knows it, too. My heavy breathing says it all. I'm barely in control of myself.

I can't let him do this.

"Yes," I say weakly. "Go, please."

It's for my own good.

"Fine." He opens the door, but turns to give me a cocky grin as he says, "But I know you're lying."

When he's gone, I slump down against the wall.

"Oh Maddy, what have you gotten yourself into?" I whisper to myself.

Chapter 6

Zane

I pull up to the shop with a huge ass grin on my face.

I fucking love how much I shocked her. That flush I saw on her cheeks makes my dick jump in my pants. I can imagine that blush on her chest, rising up to her cheeks as I pound her tight little pussy. Fuck, I want that. I groan as my dick hardens and my balls fucking hurt. I need a release. This broad has me so worked up.

Peaches. My sweet Georgia Peach. I'm definitely getting her under me. I don't give a fuck how hard she pushes me away. She wants me, and I want her.

I almost had her in her kitchen. I'm surprised she let it get that far. She's definitely losing her will to fight this. I'm enjoying it though, breaking down her walls.

I'll have to wait and play this right. I wasn't sure if she was really that sweet innocent thing I thought she was pretending to be at the bar. But she is. A little uptight, too. Which makes it all the more challenging.

"Yo, Needles!" My partner in crime turns around at the desk when I come in.

He's young. Just turned twenty-two last week, which was a fucking fabulous night out. He doesn't look it though. He's got pale blond hair and a patchy beard that looks like he's going through puberty.

Poor bastard. The clean-shaven look only makes him look that much younger. He tatted himself up pretty good to add some age to him. He did a shit job on his left arm though. That's how we met. He had to come to a professional to fix it up.

Ever since then it's been the two of us running this place. There are a few other artists working out of our shop. But we're the only ones here open to close, and we're the reason the shop is so well-known.

At first Vlad didn't like it. It's not good to be in the spotlight. But then he saw it as the perfect opportunity to launder some big accounts through here. I don't know how big, and I don't ask questions.

I set my keys on the counter and take a look around. The place is everything I ever wanted. The entrance is spacious and open with floor to ceiling windows, and a large granite-topped counter in the center. The back wall is lined with art we've done. There are four sofas, two on each side, and a coffee table in between the two sets. Photo albums of what we've done in the past sit on the table.

Two hallways lead to a total of eight rooms in the back. We're always comfortable while we're working since the other five artists helped decorate our rooms exactly how Needles and I wanted. Room six is our stockroom, and the last two are for the mob. They're always locked, and I haven't even looked in them for nearly a year. I like to forget Vlad has his hands in my shop. Some days I don't even notice when the Koranav come in and out. For the most part, we ignore them, and they ignore us.

It makes it easy for us both, and that's the way I like it.

It feels like home in here. I fucking love this place.

"What's going on?" he asks, turning from organizing a station cart. We've got all sorts of products for aftercare that the customers can buy.

He looks back over his shoulder and then does a double take. "What's going on? Why the hell are you so fucking chipper?" he asks with a grin.

"What? I can't be happy?"

"At eight in the morning? No. You're a real unpleasant fucker this early."

I laugh at him and take a seat at the counter. "Met a girl who keeps pushing me away."

He chuckles and shakes his head. "She's smart." He stands up and takes a last look at everything he's refilled. Looks good to me. I trust Needles to handle this shit. He can handle the business aspect of things.

"You take a look at your first client?" he asks and I know why, too.

"Yeah, gonna be fucking boring, but I got something fun planned later on." My first client needs a touch-up and his ink refreshed. It's fading and looking an ugly shade of green as a result. It sucks because it's mindless work, just coloring in what someone else has done. I'm gonna do some fading on it though. I'll give it a professional touch, but it's still mindless.

I hate doing those jobs almost as much as those damn anchor and butterfly tattoos. Nothing's worse than when a young girl comes in and picks a generic tat out of a book, something that I've done a thousand times. I could draw them with my eyes closed at this point.

If only I could get my hands on peaches. I bite down on the inside of my cheek thinking about how fucking smooth her skin was. I wanna press my lips against her neck and kiss down her collarbone. Farther. I'd kiss down her breasts. I know just how they'd feel in my hands.

I could put something there for her, something on the underside of her plush tits. Maybe have it travel down her side. Fuck, she'd be so fucking sexy with a touch of ink. She's got a beautiful sun-kissed tan. She'd look even more beautiful with my art on her. Not that she isn't already gorgeous.

But she's a good girl. I bet if she has anything on her body it's just some sweet little butterfly on her shoulder. And I didn't see a damn thing on her shoulder. Her tight body's just the perfect canvas for my art.

Just as I start thinking about every inch of her body and what else I'd love to do with it, Marky comes in. He's a regular. He's retired and comes in here all the time just to hang out. When we remodeled a few years ago he even did half the work. He didn't want to be paid, just wanted to be useful.

I gave him a free tat and we called it even.

I like that he comes in here just to hang out and keep us smiling. He brings a good vibe into the shop. Adds to the comfort of this place.

"Zane, Needles," he says in a gruff voice as he sets down a carrier with four coffees. He's got his own in his other hand. Trisha and Logan will be in soon to snag their coffees. Marky's pretty fucking reliable for bringing in the morning brew.

Trisha wasn't into it at first. She's a picky broad. But Marky was determined to break down her walls and it started with getting her latte right, or whatever the fuck she drinks. Out of all of us, she opens up to him first when she has something she needs to get off her chest.

"Yes!" Needles grabs his cup and doesn't even check the temperature before guzzling it down. I take mine in my hand, but I don't like mine kissed-the-fucking-sun scalding hot like he does. I vent the lid, giving it a chance to cool off some.

"Thanks, man. What are you up to today?" I ask Marky.

"Not much." Marky grabs his usual seat in the chair next to the counter. "Just needed to get out of the house this morning." He lost his wife a while back. They'd been married for nearly forty years before cancer took her from him. I know it still hurts him to live in the house they'd had together since they got married. But the stubborn fuck won't leave.

Can't say I blame him, but I don't envy him either.

"What's new with you?" he asks. "You look too fucking happy for not having had your coffee yet."

Needles snorts. "See, told you."

I look between the two of them like they've lost their damn minds. "What the fuck?"

"Just saying, you're not much of a morning person is all." Marky looks at me expectantly.

"I can't be happy?" I ask.

"Quit fucking around," he says, rolling his eyes.

"Met a girl," I say with my grin spreading into an all-out smile.

Needles laughs at me, and Marky cracks a smile.

"She's that good in bed, huh?" Needles asks as he slaps my back and sets his cup down on the counter.

The smile leaves my face. I don't wanna tell them I haven't tapped that yet. But at the same time, some part of me also kinda does. There's something about having to chase her that

I fucking love.

"She's not that kind of girl," I say before taking a sip of my coffee, trying to play this cool.

Needles looks at me incredulously. "You're hung up on a girl you haven't even had yet?" Marky chuckles at him and leans back in his seat. Needles has no fucking room to talk. I don't even know the last time he got laid. He's all talk, no game. So he can shove it.

"Fuck off," I say. "She's a challenge. I like that about her."

His brows raise. "Ten bucks says she's too good for you. Either that or she's stuck-up."

My jaw tics at his words. I don't like either of those thoughts. I also don't like that the first one is true. Yeah, she's too good for me, but good girls love bad boys. So I have a shot. Even if she thinks she can get away from me.

"What's her name?" Marky asks, snapping me back to the present.

"Madeline, but she goes by Maddy."

"Madeline is the name of a bitch with a stick up her ass," Needles immediately blurts out. He says the words confidently, and he's real close to getting his ass kicked. I don't like it. I don't like how he's thinking about her, and that it's so easy for him to talk about her like that.

"Your fucking name is Cody. I don't think you have much room to talk, you preppy jock, you." Marky laughs at the two of us. Cody Lewinsky is as far from a jock as you can get. He's lanky and goth as fuck. At first I wasn't sure I'd like him, to be honest. And he didn't talk much during our first session. Apparently, he doesn't like other people inking him. Can't blame him for that though, because I don't either. As soon as I was finished with the first session and he saw my work, he started talking and hasn't stopped since.

We bonded over our shared passion for tattooing and I really got to know him. He's a funny guy, but real standoffish. I like the fucker though. And his art is on point and on trend. That's what people go to him for, and it works out nicely for the business.

"Where'd you meet her?" Marky asks as Garret walks through the front door.

Garret Duncan is best described as Vlad's go-to henchman. He's tall and classically handsome like Jackson is, but he's fucking ruthless and coldhearted. One look at him and you can tell. What's worse is the fucker doesn't like me. He sees me as a threat because the rest of the mob is too fucking scared of me beating their asses to fuck with me.

I'm no threat though. I have no intention of being any more involved with the mob than I already am. I don't want to be Vlad's lapdog. But Garret does, and he thinks everyone's a threat to that goal. I'm just waiting for the day he steps up, thinking he can take me. I'll be ready though.

"Garret!" Needles calls out as he walks toward us. "It's in the back." He keeps his voice even, but he's tense. No one fucking likes Garret being in here. But once a week he comes to get the cash.

It's a necessity. An unfortunate one.

As Garret walks past us with a simple nod and not a single word said, I see Trisha walking toward the front door. She spots Garret and does an about-face. She fucking hates him. Trisha is short and petite, doesn't have an ounce of muscle on her. She also doesn't have any visible ink on her either. She's tatted up though. She's got a UV tat on her back. It's fucking gorgeous.

When people come in, they're surprised a cute little thing like Trisha is an artist. She went to school for ballet, for fuck's sake. She's an artist through and through. And she's damn good at her techniques. Her specialty is in unique tattooing methods. She doesn't work much because of it, but she's happy with that.

Trisha can be a strong force when push comes to shove, but she's a smart woman. She avoids conflict whenever possible. And for her that means staying away from Garret, and the rest of the mob for that matter.

She'll come back when he's gone, I'm sure. I feel for her though. She's a damn good artist and a real sweetheart. I hate that I put all of them through this shit. But I'm firmly under Vlad's thumb. There's nothing I can do to change this shit. Maybe someday if Nikolai ever takes over things will be different, but I'm not holding my breath on that one. Not with Garret in the picture.

"So?" Marky asks, and it takes a minute to remember what the hell he's talking about.

"So what?" I ask.

"The girl, Maddy?"

The tight feeling in my chest lets up and an asymmetric grin slips into place. I can't fucking stand Garret being in my shop, but I can get the fuck over shit I can't change. I don't let things I can't help keep me down. If I did, I'd be one real miserable fucker. Besides, we're used to this. It's coming on four years now of this routine. It's easier to just ignore it.

"Met her at the club the other night." I take a sip of coffee and stare at the label. "Turns out she's my neighbor." I don't tell them she took off that night and now she's stuck with me. My grin widens; her ass really is stuck with me this time.

Needles chuckles. "That's a real fucking tease."

"You're telling me." I think about how she pushed me away. She's teasing both of us. I fucking love it.

"She's a good girl and real fucking smart, too." I took a look at her books when I helped her unpack. I have to admit, the more I get to know about her, the more I like.

"Sounds like she's out of your league." Garret walks past us as Needles puts his two cents in.

Out of my league? Probably. But I still fucking want her. Besides, I'm just talking about a fuck. Every good girl likes a little taste of the bad boy.

"If she's a good girl, and she's not slumming it for the night, my money is on her staying far away from you." It's like he read my mind and he's determined to put me in a bad mood. I know how she felt with my body pressed up against hers. I know she wants me.

"What's that supposed to mean?" My fist clenches, and my brow furrows. What the fuck? Needles is like my fucking brother. He's supposed to be on my side.

"I'm saying she's too good for you." He takes a look up from the books and realizes how pissed off I am. "Not that that's a bad thing. She's probably stuck-up and wound too tight anyway."

"All 'cause her name is Madeline?" He doesn't even know her.

"No," he says in a hard voice. "'Cause you wanted her, and she turned you down. She's the bitch from the club who left you hanging, isn't she?" Fuck, I wish I hadn't told him that.

"Watch it. She's not a bitch." My voice drops low and I narrow my eyes at him. Yeah, she turned me down. Nothing fucking wrong with that. I need to take it easy and slow with her, but I'm going to have her. I fucking know I will.

He puts his hands up in surrender and gives me a look I've never seen from him before. A look as if he's scared I'm gonna kick his ass. And he should be scared. I don't like the way he's talking about her. This protective nature in me is something new to me. But I can't help it. I don't want my best friend talking about her like that.

"I'm just saying, if she doesn't like you, then that loss is on her. That's all I'm saying."

I let it slide and try to get this tension out of my shoulders and just relax. He's only looking to defend me. He doesn't like her for running off, but he doesn't know enough to judge. If he met her, things would be different. Just that simple thought calms me enough to let it all roll off my shoulders.

"Who's that?" Garret asks. As far as I'm concerned, it's none of his damn business.

"Just Zane's neighbor," Needles answers, and I wish he hadn't. I don't want Garret knowing about her. Or Vlad, for that matter. They sure as fuck don't need to know where she lives.

Garret's brows raise and a crooked grin grows on his face. I don't like it. My stomach sinks, and I have to set my coffee on the counter.

"She givin' you a hard time?" he asks with a wicked twinkle in his eyes. Both him and Vlad have been known to rough up women. That, and fuck women a little *too close* to being *too young*. My first thought is to make it very clear that I want him to stay far away from her, but I can't say that. Knowing him, he'd go after her if he knew that's what I wanted. Just to fuck with me, and just to hurt her.

"Not at all. She's just making me work for it." I try to come off casual, and I think it works.

Garret lets out a humorless laugh. "Well if you need any help taming her, I'd be happy to join in." A sickness rolls through me and Needles is quick to look away. His face is pale, and he keeps his eyes on the floor. He forgets all the fucking time who we're dealing with, and what Garret's capable of. I'm the only one in here who's a member of the Koranav. I'm the one who has to deal with these fucks. I try to keep the two separate, but I wish Needles would shut the fuck up sometimes.

Marky starts to say something, but I cut him off. "All good," I say. I'm quick to just shut it down. "If I ever need anything, I'll ask for it. But on this issue, I'm all good on my own." I hold his gaze, daring him to push any further.

He tilts his head and grins. "Alright then." I hope I didn't tempt him. I don't think I did, but I'm sure as fuck gonna be keeping a closer eye on Maddy, and Katie, too.

"Catch you boys later," Garret says. I give him a nod, still holding his gaze until he turns away.

It's quiet in the shop for a minute. I take a sip and cut Needles off as he starts to apologize to me. I shake my head and reassure him, "It's all good."

"So about this girl?" Marky asks. I stare back at him, wondering if I should even go for her. She is too good for me. I shouldn't bring her into this shit. I'll look out for those two if Garret starts coming around, but I shouldn't bring trouble to her doorstep.

"You really hung up on her?"

I cluck my tongue against the roof of my mouth. It's not

like I wanna marry her. I'm just intrigued by the challenge. And I know she wants me. I remember the way she molded her body against mine. I remember the spark between us. Fuck, yes. I need to have the broad.

I clear my throat and give Marky a small smile as my first client walks through the door. "She's a real good girl who's gonna find out what it's like to be with a bad boy like me." I give Needles a smile which finally puts him at ease.

He chuckles as he says, "Yeah, okay. I'll believe it when it happens."

Chapter 7

Madeline

For the next week, I avoid Zane like the plague. Not that I have any time to see him. My class schedule is packed, and I'm usually awake by six a.m. and home by seven p.m. on most days. I don't have much time after homework to do anything but argue with Katie over dumb shit and then turn in for sleep.

She gets on my damn nerves, but I love her. I'd be lost without her, and the same goes for her.

The bus I'm on comes to a stop a couple of blocks away from my condo. I get off after thanking the driver, mentally cursing that I didn't just wait for Katie to get out of her world history class so we could have carpooled. Though, I could have just taken the car home myself and left Katie there to take the bus.

I would have never heard the end of it, I think to myself. *Besides, riding on the bus wasn't that bad.*

That's one thing I hate about sharing a car in a strange town. I can't move about like I want. I'd love to go find a coffee shop and open my books up and just relax as I study. I used to do that all the time back home. The walkability in my town was fabulous. Not here though. For a state college there's literally nothing around it. Main Street has four stores on it. Four! I'm not used to being so far away from shops. I wanna get out and go somewhere to unwind.

I smile as I remember the purchases I made before I left campus. Thank God one of those stores was a liquor shop. A glass of wine will make this economics homework far more enjoyable. Or at least less miserable.

The whole ride home I'd been thinking about the scene in the kitchen with Zane. How hot his body felt against mine, how much I wanted him to take me right then and there, and how close I'd come to giving myself over to him totally.

That would certainly make my night more entertaining. And God knows I need some sort of release. Badly. And soon.

Now my panties are soaking wet, and I can't wait to get home to change out of them. Inwardly I curse Zane for my affliction. If he would just stay away from me, I wouldn't be spending half my time thinking naughty thoughts and fighting my desire for him. I'm starting to wonder why I'm even fighting him. It's not like it'd be the worst thing in the world to give in a little. He'd be a distraction though. Not like a coffee shop where I could just pick up and leave whenever I wanted.

I can already tell he'd be an addiction. And then when I was at his mercy and begging for his touch, he'd break me. Yeah, that's why I need to stay away.

By the time I turn the corner and the condo comes into view, I'm tired. I've been walking across campus all day and the bookbag I'm carrying feels like it weighs a ton. My shoulders feel sore.

I'm halfway to the condo when I hear, "You look like you had a rough day, peaches." The deep voice sends a chill down my spine, and I have to close my eyes.

Is this guy a ghost or something? Seriously, he always seems to appear without warning.

I turn to see Zane standing there with that cocky smirk on his face. His hair is slicked back, he's wearing blue jeans, and a white, short-sleeved shirt that shows off his bulging biceps and tattoos. Tatted and ripped. That describes him perfectly.

I don't know what it is, but he seems to get hotter every time I see him, I think, practically salivating over the sexy bad boy.

I scowl at him to hide my lust, letting him know he's nothing special.

"Where did you come from?" I demand coolly. I'm sure as shit not going to let him know how he really affects me. He'd only try harder if he knew how I've started thinking about him at night. His bedroom is right across from mine, and I'm ashamed to admit how I've peeked through my curtains a time or two. I've already decided we need to move when this lease is up.

Zane twists his chiseled features into a mocking pout. "Damn, I don't get a 'Hi, how are you?'"

I cross my arms across my breasts. "No," I say flatly. I want to say, *I'm not going to be nice to you when you make me feel so... sexually frustrated.* "Sorry." I tack on the sorry and only partly feel like a complete bitch. I need to push this guy away. He's no good for me. If that means I have to be a bitch, so be it. He'll get the hint and leave me alone.

Zane lets out a mock sigh. "Damn, and here I was thinking that you couldn't wait to kiss me."

Despite pretending to be bitchy, Zane seems to sense I want to kiss him. Badly.

It only further irritates me.

"No, what I can't wait to do, is go inside my condo and take a nice hot shower."

Zane's right eyebrow shoots up. "A hot shower, huh?"

I curse inwardly for making myself an easy target, my face flaming from his implication. "Yeah, now out of my way." I barge on past Zane, intent on leaving him in the dust. But he's not about to let me get away, walking me down in two quick strides. Come on! What do I have to do to get him to pick on someone else?

"Not so fast, peaches. Let me handle that load for you." Without asking, he removes my bookbag from my shoulders. My arms slip the loops before I can stop them, and I whip around to face him. I swear sparks penetrate my shirt when his hands get near me.

"Better now?" he asks.

I open my mouth to say a biting reply, but then close it. Despite his playfulness, Zane is only being a gentleman to me, and I'm treating him like crap. Maybe I should stop being so abrasive toward him and give him a chance.

But that's what he wants, I argue with myself. *For me to let my guard down so he can get in. If he's being nice, it's only because he wants to win this little game since I'm probably the first girl that's turned him down in years, and he can't handle it.*

I do have to admit my shoulders feel a lot better without the heavy weight on them.

"Yes," I say grudgingly as I roll my shoulders. "But you didn't have to do that. The condo is right there."

"I didn't *have* to, but I wanted to." He seems so sincere that I immediately feel guilty.

I look away and give him a small, "Thank you. I really appreciate it."

"Anything for a pretty lady," he says, lightening up the mood.

I snort. "Please."

"Why do you always give me such a rough time? I'm just

trying to get to know you."

"Because you're bad news," I say, "and knowing you is probably more trouble than it's worth." I have to be honest. Maybe if he knows what I'm thinking, he'll respect my decision and leave me alone.

Zane makes a hurt face. "Why do you have such a low opinion of me? What have I done to deserve it?"

I gesture at him. "Just look at you. You look like trouble in the flesh, the good looks, the tattoos. You have such a... bad boy vibe."

"Hey, there's nothing wrong with being a bad boy. And since when did being good-looking and having tattoos become a crime?"

"Don't try to sit here and act like you aren't a player that hasn't been with a billion girls and doesn't have several girlfriends right now."

"I don't," Zane says. I don't fucking believe that, and I don't do liars. I *hate* liars.

"Sure." *I bet he probably has ten packs of Trojans in his pocket right now. The extra large kind.*

"What will it take for you to believe me?" he asks, and I don't even look at him when I answer.

"Nothing."

"Come on, you can do better than that. Ask me anything you want about my personal life, and I'll give you a truthful answer."

As much as I want to grill Zane on his past, I don't want

to seem like I'm too interested. Besides, I doubt he'll tell me the truth about his sexual escapades. "I don't have to ask anything. You're a player, and that's all I need to know." The scene from the other night with the bartender flashes in front of my eyes, the way she looked as if she wanted Zane to fuck her right then and there.

I wonder if he's already been with her. She knew his name. *He must be good if she wanted seconds.*

"Okay. You got me. Yes, I've been with a lot of girls, and yes I haven't been a model citizen. But I can swear to you that I don't have any secret girlfriends or anything like that. In fact, you're the first girl in a long time that's intrigued me."

"I'm the first girl in a long time that's resisted your advances, you mean," I say bitchily before I can stop myself.

"Yeah, that too, and I can't lie, it makes me want to get to know you."

I knew it, I think to myself. *He's only after me because I haven't fallen at his feet like all the other girls in his life.* The second I do, he'll drop me like a bad habit.

Decision decided. There's no way I'm letting my guard down for him.

"Thanks for proving my point." I don't know why, but I wanna cry. It hurts thinking I was right about him. I knew it though.

"That doesn't prove shit," Zane growls. He seems irritated with my assumptions about him. I must say, he looks even sexier when he's angry. "And it has zero to do with whether I'm looking for a quick hookup. Which I'm not."

"Bullshit. The way you've pushed me up against the wall, twice I might add, suggests otherwise." As annoyed as I am, just thinking about our close encounters sends goosebumps up my arm and makes my clit throb.

Zane gives me an intense look that makes butterflies flutter in my stomach. "But you liked it. And you wanted it."

I open my mouth to swear at him in denial, but then snap it shut. It's true. I did like it. And boy, do I fucking want it. But luckily, I have enough wits about me to know that nothing good would come from doing the sideways tango with him.

"Sorry, I don't know what you're talking about," I say. My cheeks heat and he smirks at me. Damn it. Now *I'm* a liar.

"Don't lie, peaches. You just need to give me a chance, get to know me. All I need is one night with you to change your perception of me."

"Never," I swear, though inwardly I'm trembling at the prospect of having one night with Zane.

We reach the doorstep of my condo and I stop to stare at him. "Well?" I ask. I just need to get my bag. Have some wine and study. I need to focus.

He knows exactly what I mean, but he plays coy. "Well, what?"

I hold out my hand. "Give me my bookbag back so I can

go inside," I order flatly.

Grinning, he keeps my bag out of reach. "What's the magic word?"

"Now!" I growl.

"Eeenh. Wrong."

I place my hands on my hips and give him the most murderous scowl I can manage. "I'm not saying it, so you can either give me my bag back, or you can get the hell out of my way."

He studies me, and I have the distinct feeling that he's loving my sass, judging by that cocky grin on his face. "You're a stubborn little peach, aren't ya?" he remarks, his eyes twinkling.

I continue to scowl at him. "Will you stop calling me that? It's friggin' annoying."

"You know you love it."

I hate to admit it, but his little nickname is growing on me. I'll be damned if I let him know that though.

"In your dreams."

"Indeed." He lets out a mock sigh when I remain unmoved. "Alright peaches, being the nice guy that I am, and even after how rude you've treated me, I'll let you slide with no apology--"

"Good--" I say, interrupting before he can finish. I try to snatch my bag out of his hands, but he evades me easily and says, "If you go on a date with me."

My jaw drops like a bridge during a siege. Zane just isn't

going to take no for an answer. "Are you serious?" I should be flattered, but instead I'm shocked. And maybe a little scared. How long is he going to keep pursuing me? If he just wants another notch on his headboard, he could easily find someone else.

He nods. "I'll take you somewhere nice and show you I'm not the bad guy you think I am."

"No," I say after a moment. "I don't want to go on a date with you. Not now. Not ever."

Zane is shocked by my refusal, though he tries to hide it, and he stares at me for the longest time before finally saying, "As you wish." He comes forward and gently places my bag in my hand.

I snarl, "Thank you. Now have a nice day." I move to walk past him, when suddenly he grabs me and pushes me up against the front door.

"I didn't say that you could go in yet," he growls, his breath hot on my neck. Apparently he's not as shocked as he looked by my rejection. I'm doing a shit job at hiding how much he turns me on.

Why do I keep winding up in the same position? I wonder. Once again, I'm sandwiched between Zane's hard body and a hard place. And once again, I'm turned on to the max.

Oh fuck, I can feel his erection digging into my side. Shit, shit. My pussy clenches. A primal side of me wants him to take me like this and fuck me against the door for being so rude to him. I bite my lip and feel my core heat for him.

His lips are so close to mine and I want nothing more than to kiss them, suck on them. Devour them. Down below, my pussy clenches again with longing. I'd let him punish me with that thick cock of his. This is bad. Why does he keep doing this to me?

Zane stares into my eyes, and I'm suddenly lost in his. All I can think to myself is, *Why am I resisting this hot ass man? Just give in. Let him take me. All of me*

Yes!

By now I'm hyperventilating, burning up with desire. I feel like all my defenses are crumbling, like I'm a few moments away from being totally his. And I want it. I want him.

Zane knows this too and he gives me an arrogant grin. He moves in close, bringing his lips close to my neck. I can feel his hot breath on it and it's driving me wild, making my limbs shudder with anticipation.

Take me, I groan inwardly. *Take me right here. Right now.*

Zane trails his lips up my neck, grazing my flesh, all the way to mine. This is it. This is the moment he kisses me and I give in to him.

Ready to finally surrender, I close my eyes and wait, my breathing ragged.

A second later, Zane lets out a mocking laugh and I pop them back open.

"Sorry peaches, but I gotta go," he says, releasing me and

stepping away.

I gasp as fury twists the insides of my stomach. The bastard just made a fool out of me!

"If you want to take me up on my offer, you know where to find me," he says in parting. As he walks off, he's wearing a cocky smile that says, *Payback is a bitch.*

In anger, I watch him walk over to his condo and disappear inside, leaving me feeling sexually frustrated. Again.

Chapter 8

Zane

I lean my head into the spray of hot water and run my hands through my hair. The water feels good, but it's not doing a damn thing for this erection Maddy left me with. I rinse my body, feeling a million times better now that I have the sweat of the day off of me. I got in the shower as soon as I was done helping her loosen up some. But fuck, what I need is definitely not a shower.

I almost have Maddy where I want her. She was so close. But she would have regretted anything I'd done to her. I know she would have.

And that's something I don't want. She's gonna be right next door to me. She can't get away from me, but I also can't get away from her.

It'll be nice once I finally get her impaled on my dick, but I need to make sure she's gonna be happy about it afterward. I have to admit, it felt fucking good teasing her, too. It felt real good, knowing she wanted me and leaving her to suffer with her little pussy in need. My dick jumps with the need to satisfy that itch for her.

My sweet little peach is too fucking stubborn. I know she wants this. But something's holding her back.

'Cause I'm a bad man. And she's too fucking good for me.

Anger rises up as I have the thought.

Maybe that's true, but she still wants this. And I can give her the release she desperately needs.

I walk out of the shower and feel the hot steam that's filled the room. I grab a towel and pat down my face and dry off my hair. I'm too fucking hot. I almost move the towel to my waist to cover myself out of habit.

But then I remember that she's right there.

Maddy's condo is parallel to mine. Our bathrooms are right across from one another. I'm sure she could see me from her bedroom, too. I lift the blinds and open the window. There's a few feet between the buildings, so it's possible that someone walking by could see, but it's real fucking unlikely.

If my girl is in her room, I bet she could get a good look.

I look down at my cock and stroke it a few times, I need it to look good. I lean against the wall and pump my cock until it's hard as steel. I think about how her breasts felt pressed against my chest, those soft moans that spilled from her lips, and that's all I fucking need.

Shit, precum's leaking out. It's been weeks since I've had a release. I need one bad. If she'd just let me in I could be over there in a heartbeat and have both us cumming like we need to.

I open the blinds and smile wide when I see her on her bed with a large ass textbook in her lap. Yes! I open the window as far as it'll go, my thighs hitting the windowsill, and I smirk when I see her head turn to me from the corner of my eye. I pretend like I don't see her though. As if I just open my window stark fucking naked all the time. She doesn't know I don't.

Knowing how she's trying to push me away, there's no way she'd ever do this if she knew that I knew she was watching.

Damn it's hard keeping the cocky smile off my face. I turn to my side and stroke my dick once. I hear her little gasp, but I make sure I don't look out the window. In my periphery I wait for her to get up and close the curtains, but she doesn't.

Fuck yeah, my girl likes what she sees.

My forearm rests against the wall and my face is just barely showing in the window. Just enough to take a peek at her, but she can still see the goods. And judging by her face, she's happy with the merchandise.

I feel fucking cocky, knowing a girl like her is being so bad just so she can have a look at me. I let out a small groan that she can hear, and stroke my dick nice and slow.

Her eyes widen and search for mine, but I keep my face hidden in the crook of my arm.

I can practically see the wheels turn as she considers what she should do.

Be a good girl and touch yourself for me. Come on Maddy, be my sweet little peach and give me something to work with. Fuck, I wish. But that's way too much for me to hope for.

She's a smart girl, I bet she knows what I'm up to. I can see the hesitation, but more than that, lust. For a second I think she's going to leave, or get up and close her curtains. But she doesn't.

She watches as I stroke myself for her. I angle my body so she can see how I'm trimmed up and she can have a better angle of that sexy "V" at my hips. I've been told more than a time or two that it's my best feature. I'm pulling out everything I have to show her what I've got. Fuck, I'm peacocking like a bitch, but I don't care. I want her drooling over me and wanting me more than she's ever wanted anything else.

Seeing that heat in her eyes makes it worth it. No fucking shame at all.

Fuck me. She moves the book off her lap and leans back against the bed. Yes!

I stroke myself again as another bead of precum leaks out. I use it to rub along my head, and I swear to God her lips part with a moan and her tongue licks along her lower lip.

Yes, fuck yes. That's my girl. Let loose, baby. My peach

needs to unwind.

I picture her licking the seam of my dick, and I stroke myself faster.

I see her hand slip under the covers and I almost lose it. Fuck, that's so hot. She's so goddamned turned on by what I'm doing she has to touch herself.

I imagine myself on top of her right fucking now. I'd slip that tank top off her body and suck her hardened nubs into my mouth. I wanna feel the weight of those tits in my hand. I can hear her moan as I twirl my tongue and bite down slightly. I keep up my strokes and rub the bit of precum over the head of my dick.

Fuck, she'd feel so good. Her mouth, her pussy. I want it all. I want to feel how good she is when she cums on my dick.

I look out of the corner of my eye and she sees me. Her hand stops, and her mouth parts. She's been caught in the act. I turn to her and stroke myself again.

"Pinch your nipple," I mouth to her and she stares back at me. Right now's not a time for teasing. I can't fucking take another standoff ending with both of us still hot and bothered. I need to cum, she needs it, too.

I tilt my head down and stare straight into her eyes.

"Do it. Now," I tell her. I know she wants this. It's now or never, peaches. Don't disappoint me.

Her left hand moves to her tank top and she pinches her nipple quickly through her shirt and lets her hand fall after that. I smirk at her. I'm not letting her get off that easy.

I shake my head. "Let me see." I stroke myself again and her eyes fall to my dick.

Fuck me, she licks her lips and her hand moves under the sheet. I should let her have this. I know I should. I could scare her away by taking control, but I need to push.

I clear my throat, drawing her attention back to me.

"I wanna see." She bites her bottom lip as a flush moves up her chest and into her cheeks. She looks so vulnerable, so damn beautiful. She nods her head and slowly pulls the strap of her tank top down, exposing her plump, milky breasts and small, pert nipples. Fuck, I want my mouth on her right now. For a second I think about going over there. But I don't want to risk losing her. I feel like the second I lose eye contact she's gonna run far away from me. I need to make sure she gets off.

"Pinch it," I mouth. She's slow to move, but she obeys. That in and of itself is an accomplishment. Finally, she listens to me. She gently pinches her nipple, rolling it between her finger.

"Again." She keeps eye contact and pinches it again before taking the other strap down and doing the same to her other nipple.

Fuck, I'm so close to cumming. This broad has me wrapped around her finger and she doesn't even know it.

"Harder." I give her the command and she moves both her hands to her nipples, but I shake my head.

"One hand. Play with yourself." She stares at me for a

moment and I wonder if she heard me right. But then she slips her hand back down.

"I wanna see." That right there is the line. She shakes her head and the same fear I keep seeing in her eyes is there. I stop my movements and consider going over there right now and showing her how fucking good it's gonna be when she surrenders to me, but then I think twice.

This is a broad who needs time and space. I have to earn her trust. I can give her that. I can show her she can trust me.

I repeat my words, "I wanna see you." She shakes her head slightly and I don't push for more. "Don't stop, peaches." I stroke myself again. "Cum with me."

She's slow to move, but after a long moment she does. And I feel so much fucking relief that she does.

That's my girl.

I start pumping my cock, watching her ease back against her headboard.

She spreads her legs wider under the covers, but she leaves the blanket there covering herself.

Even covered, she's beautiful and tempting in every way. Maybe even more so since she's still hiding from me.

"Again." I give the command aloud and her eyes widen, darting to the narrow path between our buildings, but there's no one there, only us in this moment.

She bites down on her lip and pinches her nipple hard. Yes. Fuck, yes. I quicken my pace and give her another order.

"More." *More.* That's what I want from her. More of whatever she'll give me. I give her the command and watch as her back arches from how intense her touch is. I wish I were there. I wish I was the one giving her that pleasure.

I watch as her head tilts back, and her orgasm rips through her body. Her lips part and I faintly hear her moan as she cums from her own touch. It's the hottest thing I've ever seen.

My spine tingles and my balls draw up. Oh, fuck. *Maddy.* I moan her name as I cum. I cum violently, leaving a mess everywhere as hot streams pour into my hand.

I breathe out deep and look up just in time to see her pulling the curtains closed and I have to smile.

The next time I cum, it'll be inside her pretty little pussy, that's for fucking sure.

Chapter 9

Madeline

"God, I can't decide what I wanna wear," Katie complains, twisting sideways to look at her ass in my bedroom mirror. I'm sitting on my bed, having watched her complain for the past twenty minutes as we get ready for class. I think what she's wearing, blue jeans and a colorful blouse, is fine, but for some reason Katie simply can't take my advice. She's tried on at least ten different outfits and each one has something wrong with it.

"For the millionth time," I say with exasperation, Just wear that. You look fine." I don't know why she insists on asking for my advice if she isn't going to listen to me. But then again I don't know why she keeps coming in here, knowing

I'm going to say the same thing. She's looked perfectly fine in everything I've seen so far.

Katie is still twisted to one side. "I would, Maddy, but it makes my ass look flat."

"But it is." I hide my smile. She does have a flat ass. She's got a skinny waist and wide hips I admire though.

Katie turns to glare daggers at me. "What did you just say?"

"Your ass *is* flat," I clarify. "Flat as a pancake." I don't let on that I'm fucking with her, partly to get back at her for keeping me prisoner while she tries on her entire wardrobe.

Katie rushes forward, grabs a pillow off the bed and lobs it at my head. "Bitch."

I dodge it, giggling. "I'm only kidding!"

Katie crosses her arms over her breasts and scowls. "No you're not!"

"I am. I swear." I put my hands up in surrender, but apparently she's really pissed off.

"I don't believe you, Miss Evil. But you know what? Your ass isn't exactly anything special either, so there." Katie sticks her tongue out at me.

"Oh honey," I warn, "don't go there."

"Why not? You just did." Touché. But I didn't say it to hurt her. I'll try being honest with her, see if that doesn't make her less pissy.

"I only said it to get you to stop complaining."

"That worked out well, didn't it?" she asks with a bitchy

tone. What the ever loving fuck? She better be kidding.

"It stopped you from complaining, didn't it?" I point out.

Katie sighs. "I knew I should have picked Vanessa for my roommate. She would have never had the nerve to tell me I have a flat ass."

"Hey!" I protest.

Katie sticks her tongue out at me again. "Now you see how it feels."

I cluck my tongue. "You need to get laid." She's either PMSing or seriously deprived of sexual gratification.

"*You* need to get laid. I can't believe you pushed Zane away for a second time."

If only you knew what happened last night, I think to myself. While I told Katie about my episode with Zane in the kitchen, she has no idea about our encounter the previous day, and I'm not sure if I'm going to tell her about that. *Or how close I am to having wild, crazy sex with him.*

"Have you seen him at all since moving day?" she asks, interrupting my thoughts.

Oh yeah. I've more than seen him.

Images of his naked, hard, chiseled body and big, fat fucking cock flash in my mind and my temperature starts to rise as I relive the events from the previous day. It felt so good to relieve some of that tension that had been building since we first met. Still, there's a lot of tension left, and down below, my pussy starts to feel moist and my clit throbs. In vain, I try to push these naughty thoughts away, cursing how horny they make me.

"Are you okay?" Katie asks, peering at me with concern.

"Huh?" I say breathlessly. I'm literally in a daze. Seriously, I'm about two seconds away from shoving Katie out of the room and spending some quality time with my rabbit, my favorite vibrator.

"I asked if you'd seen Zane."

"Oh. Nope," I lie. "I haven't seen him."

Katie frowns with disappointment. "It's a shame you won't give him a chance. I'd kill to have a guy that hot that crazy over me."

"Why would you? You'd be killing for a guy who probably has several different girlfriends that don't even know about each other." And that's it right there. I know he can have anyone he wants. There's nothing special about me except that I keep pushing him away. So the moment I sleep with him, it'll be over and I'll be crushed. It's a horrible fucking position to be in... because I *really* wanna fuck him.

Katie taps her fingers against her chin. "You know what? You're probably right."

"I know I am."

"I still wouldn't let that stop me from having at least one night with him. Shit, if I were you, I'd be over there riding him right now." She grins wickedly, as if imagining all the naughty things she'd be doing with Zane. "Some early morning foreplay before class."

"Katie!" I flush. Shit, I'd love that. And he's right there. He's so close.

Katie makes her customary fake innocent face. "Wha?"

I smack a palm against my forehead, and shake my head. "Nevermind. I just can't with you."

Despite my objection, I can't help but think about what Katie said. How I would love to be over there right now, riding Zane's big fat cock, feeling him pump those powerful hips beneath me, thrusting deep inside of me with powerful force. My clit throbs in response to my fantasy, and I unconsciously touch myself.

"Maddy?" Katie asks, looking closely at me with curiosity.

I snatch my hand away from my lower stomach, my heart pounding, shocked by how close I've come to touching my muff in front of my best friend.

Screw you Zane, I rage, *for making me feel this way, for making me lose control.*

I have no idea how I'm going to get through the day with all these dirty thoughts running through my mind. There is no way I'll be able to focus. I might as well stay home.

This is why getting with a guy like Zane is no good. We're not even an item yet and he's already affecting my school performance. And my sanity.

"Yeah?" I say, trying to play it cool.

"You alright?" she asks with a cocked brow.

"Yeah, why?" I clear my throat and can't even look her in the eyes.

Katie shook her head. "I dunno, you started panting and looking all funny and then you were reaching down for your... umm... hoohaw. Got a yeast infection?"

I scowl with indignation. "Heck no!"

"Oh. Because I do," she says with a shrug.

"Okay, that's TMI."

"Why?" Katie complains. "Aren't we besties that are supposed to share everything together? Anyway, it itches like hell! I was scratching my stuff so much this morning that my labia turned all--"

"Katie!" I yell.

"Wha?"

"TMI!"

We spend the next ten minutes arguing over whether Katie should just wear what she has on or change into another outfit until I point out that if we don't leave soon, we'll wind up late for class. After a quick breakfast of Corn Pops and OJ, we walk outside.

It's a cool morning, the sun is radiant, and the sky is crystal clear. It's beautiful. It's so pretty here. It doesn't have the walkability of being in the city, but I'm starting to love this place.

"It's a beautiful day today, isn't?" Katie echoes my sentiment.

I'm about to respond when something that's even more

beautiful appears out of the condo next door. His hair slicked back, Zane looks like he's stepped out of GQ magazine with his dark pants and dress shirt that's opened at the chest, exposing the tanned bronze skin underneath. I swear I can see my tongue rolling along the lines of his chest. His shoulders are so broad, the shirt stretches tight over his muscles. Fuck, he's so hot.

With swagger to die for, Zane walks up to us with a playboy grin on his face. It's hard to look him in the eyes. I just want to stare at his dick, as if it's out on display again.

I'm not sure what the protocol is for watching your neighbor masturbate, but my plan is to just ignore it and hope he doesn't say shit about it. I'm just going to pretend like it never happened.

He better not say anything. My heart beats faster in my chest. I can see him teasing me for it. Holding it over my head. Shit! And then Katie will know I lied. Fuck, he better not.

"Are you stalking me now?" I demand, trying to act cool and confident when I'm really shaking inside. All I can think about as I look at him is how hot he looks naked and about his big fat, pulsating cock.

"Hey," Katie protests, "you don't have to be so rude to Zane, Maddy. Geez."

Unperturbed, Zane chuckles, a deep throaty sound that does strange things to my nether regions. "Don't be so vain, peaches, I have to work, too."

I snort. "Well those are some pretty nice clothes just for a tattoo parlor."

"What can I say? I like looking good."

And you smell good too, I think to myself. Zane's wearing a spicy cologne that turns me on big time. I wanna know what it is. I think I read somewhere that we remember scents the most out of all the senses. I wanna remember this smell. It's like a masculine scent that was made just for him.

I'm stumped for a comeback. I'd be lying if I say he looks bad, because he looks like sex on legs. Hell, he's practically a sex god, Zane Adonis Whatever-the-fuck-his-last-name-is.

Katie giggles. "Dude, you look more than good, like a million bucks!"

I shoot Katie a murderous glare for her treachery. She's supposed to be on my side.

Zane grins at Katie's compliment and then says, "But maybe I did decide to leave the second you came out."

"See. You're a stalker." I hold back my smile and the small thrill I get from him admitting it. It shouldn't make me so freaking happy, but it does.

"But I won't have to be one if you'd just hang out with me, preferably by watching a movie or something."

Katie leans in and growls into my ear, "Maddy, if you don't say yes, I'm going to possess your body and have violent sex with him." I have to laugh from her threat.

I'm silent for almost a full minute, my mind racing, before

I finally say, "Fine. You win. I'll hang out with you."

Victory flashes in Zane's eyes, but he's not surprised. He knew I would give in eventually, the arrogant bastard. "A movie at your place it is. What movie would you like to see?"

"I heard Deadpool is good," Katie chimes in.

I turn to Katie and scold, "He didn't ask you!" I turn back to Zane and deadpan. "Deadpool."

Zane laughs while Katie mutters something under her breath about finding a place to hide a dead body.

After Katie and I exchange a few more feisty barbs, Zane says, "You girls are hilarious, but I gotta get going. Got a busy schedule up at the shop." He nods at Katie and says, "See ya." And to me, "Catch you later, peaches." I blush at his words and tuck my hair back behind my ear. Shit. This is not good. He's really affecting me now. Shit!

Katie squeals with delight as we watch him walk off. "Peaches! I just love that nickname. It's so frickin' cute."

I roll my eyes. "Oh please, it's obnoxious you mean." No it's not. I fucking love it. Damn it.

Katie turns to me, a big grin on her face. "You know why he named you that, right?"

"No, why?"

"Because he wants to eat you out."

I smack Katie on the arm and she howls with laughter. "I'm so done with you, Katie Butler!"

"I'm serious. He thinks you taste sweet, and he probably

thinks about your juices, rolling down his chin while he's in between your..."

I plug my fingers in my ears. "I'm taking the bus!"

Katie laughs even harder, going red in the face.

"It's not funny!"

"Oh yes it is. You should've seen your face!"

I roll my eyes and walk off to the car. A few minutes later, we're driving down the road toward the university.

"Will you watch the movie with us and be my third wheel?" I ask, interrupting Katie in the middle of singing a Katy Perry song. It's gonna be bad if I don't have her there. I already know it. I'm ready to cave. I can't let it happen. I'm... I'm scared. That's the truth, and I'm embarrassed to admit it, but I am. I'm so scared that I'm on the edge of a cliff, and he's gonna fuck me and then throw me off.

Katie glances over at me. "Hmm. I dunno, Maddy. You've been pretty awful to me."

"I have? How?" She actually sounds hurt, and that worries me. I feel like I'm losing myself; I can't lose her, too.

"Well, let's see here, you said I have a flat ass."

"I already said that was a joke."

"And you didn't want to hear about my itchy vag." Okay, now I know she's joking. Thank fuck.

When I open to my mouth to curse, Katie holds up a hand. "Okay, okay, don't pull out your machete. I might watch with you."

"Might? What do you mean *might*?" I make sure to put a hint of a threat in my voice, because I *need* her there.

"I just don't understand why you would want me there. I mean, the guy is hot as all hell. I wouldn't want to share him in the least."

"That's the very reason why I need you to come. To keep me from doing something I regret. I mean, we're going to be in the living room on the couch together, all alone and in the dark..." My voice trails off as I think about how hot the setting sounds. I could just imagine us on the couch, Zane's lips on my neck, my hands stroking his rock-hard cock through his jeans. Just thinking about it makes my body shudder with anticipation.

"That sounds like the beginning of a porno movie."

"Katie," I growl.

"Alright, alright. I'll be there."

I lean across my seat and give Katie a brief hug. "Thank you, Katie." She really has no idea how much this means to me.

Katie looks over at me and winks as she says, "You're welcome... peaches."

I resist the urge to kill her and settle on a death glare.

Chapter 10

Zane

Fuck, I don't think I've ever been nervous like this before. It's stupid. It's not like I'm some dumb kid trying to get laid for the first time. But that same anxiety is racing through my blood.

Maybe it's the challenge? The fact that I don't *know* this is going to end in a good fuck.

That's gotta be why I'm so damn nervous. I wanna make sure I do this shit right so she'll give me more. 'Cause I sure as fuck want it.

I did my homework. I've got a funny movie she's gonna love, Deadpool. I heard the guy gets pegged though, not sure how I feel about that. And I picked out some flowers for my girl. She seems like a girl who'd like sunflowers.

Something about her tells me she'd like them more than other kinds of flowers.

I almost went traditional with a dozen red roses, but I think she'd like these better. I fucking hope she does.

I knock on the door and wait. I look down at the flowers. Shit, this is stupid.

I've never fucking bought flowers for a girl in my entire life.

I almost chuck them behind the bushes, but then the door opens.

My jaw drops slightly and my heartbeat slows.

She looks fucking gorgeous. She's in a shift dress that fades from white to pink and ends mid-thigh. It's not hugging her body, it's loose. I could rip that up and off of her in a second flat. She's teasing me by hiding her curves under that dress, but I already know how voluptuous she is.

My lips kick up into a smirk as I ask, "You get dressed up just for me, peaches?" I have to tease her. It wouldn't be the same if I didn't.

She looks like she's going to say something smart, but then she sees the flowers. She blushes a bit and rocks back on her heels. "Did you really get me flowers?"

The way her voice softens and color rises into her cheeks, I think I struck something in her. A chink in her armor. Fuck yes, sunflowers are my new favorite flower. Not that I already had one to begin with. But if I can get her guard down with a bouquet, I'll get one for her every day.

I hold them out for her to take and then lean in. My hands grip the door jamb and I take a peek inside.

"You letting me in?" I cock a brow and wait for my words to sink in.

Her smile falls comically and she rolls her eyes before turning her back to me and walking straight back toward the living room. "I'll take that as a yes."

I take a step in and close the door behind me. Her place is the mirror opposite of mine.

Except it's littered with Ikea furniture and girly shit.

"Hi Zane!" Katie bounds down the stairs with a bright smile on her face. "You're looking scrumptious today," she adds with a wink. This girl is ridiculous, but I love how Maddy whips around and gives her the evil eye. My girl's a bit jealous. Usually that's a turnoff, but on her, I fucking love it.

"Hey there, Katie," I greet. My brow furrows as I watch her swing around the staircase and head in the wrong fucking direction. What's this shit? She's gotta get her ass upstairs or preferably out of the house. The only reason I even suggested we do this here is because I knew Maddy would flat-out say no to a movie date at my place.

I walk back to the living room and find Katie taking a seat on a slipper chair in the far corner and Maddy walking into the room with the sunflowers in a vase. She sets it down on the coffee table and completely ignores my look as she walks back to the kitchen.

The look that's saying, *What the fuck is your roommate staying here for?* Katie pulls a throw blanket over her lap, completely ignoring me, too.

Maddy walks back in with two bowls of popcorn. They've got red and white stripes on them, obviously meant for movie dates. She hands one to Katie, who's apparently in charge of the remotes.

I follow Maddy to the sofa, choosing my battles. Specifically, choosing not to make this a battle. She's sitting under a blanket with a bowl of popcorn on her lap continuing to pretend she can't feel my eyes boring into her skull.

"You're gonna miss it if you don't sit down." Maddy doesn't even make eye contact with me as she says it.

If that's the way she wants to play it, fine by me. Katie's in for a show then.

I toss Katie the movie, giving in to this little battle. "All yours," I tell her.

She grins, loving that she gets to stay for this showdown. That girl is trouble and she fucking knows it.

I take my seat next to Maddy and spread my arms out over the back of the sofa. I don't even mention the obvious.

A few minutes tick by of Maddy and Katie exchanging small talk as Katie fast forwards to the start of the movie. I just watch, letting them get comfortable. The two of them take covert glances at me occasionally. I keep a smile on my face so they know I'm fine with this.

Honestly, it's fine with me. It's not gonna be fine for Maddy in a minute. But for right now, it's all good.

I try to look straight ahead and watch the movie. My peaches is leaning against the armrest, her feet are a few inches from me and she's got the blanket over her lap.

I have to figure out a way to play my next move right.

I'm sure as shit not gonna be a good boy and stay seated during the movie and have her kick my ass out as soon as it's over.

Fuck that! That's not a date. And she promised me a date.

I pick her legs up and put them on my lap. I have to hold in a laugh as a piece of popcorn falls from her mouth and lands on the floor. I've obviously startled her. She looks back at me nervously, eyeing me up and down. I keep my hands on her calves and start giving her a massage. My thumb kneads into her muscles, not too deep. Just enough to give her a soothing touch.

I wait for her to say something. To tell me to stop, but she doesn't.

Katie laughs at something we both missed. I look at the screen and a dude's getting shot.

I look back at Katie, that fucking psycho. She's cracking up.

I shake my head and grin. I look at Maddy and see she's picking at the bits of popcorn left in her bowl.

I'm quick to take it out of her hands and lay it down on the floor. She doesn't need another distraction. As I set it down I slide in behind her so my chest is to her back. She's stiff at first, but she gives in to me.

Yes, good girl. Progress.

She clears her throat and tries to lean away from me slightly. That's fine, she can play like that.

I slip my hand under the covers and rest it on her thigh. I don't squeeze, and it's on her outer thigh and over her dress. As if it's just a simple touch and there's no intention of going further. Her breathing picks up, and she knows exactly what I'm doing.

She turns against me and opens that smart mouth of hers, but I cut her off before she says anything.

"Shh, the movie's on." I keep my eyes on the screen as Katie turns.

"Hush, Maddy." I can't help the rough chuckle and wide smile as Katie admonishes Maddy.

Maddy presses her lips into a tight line and backs her ass up hard into my dick.

Oh, damn. I bend over her body slightly and hold my breath for a second. "That was real fucking close, peaches," I whisper in her ear.

She turns back to give me some of that lip, but Katie cuts her off.

"Guys!"

Maddy looks back at Katie likes she's ready to snap. I fucking love this. It's more entertaining than any movie I could've picked out.

I take advantage of the two of them engaging in a stareoff and slip my hand up Maddy's dress.

Katie gets a sly look on her face and whips her head to the TV. I'm sure my girl gave it away. But I don't give a fuck.

She arches her back as I move my hand to her pussy. The sight of her pushing her breasts out like that makes my dick even harder.

Her eyes go wide and I lean in close to her, resting my head just behind hers.

"Shh," I tell her and plant a kiss on her neck.

Her breathing picks up, but she lets me. She looks back at me and bites her lip, but she doesn't say anything.

Yes!

I tap her thighs, waiting to see if she'll let me go farther, and she does. My girl must need this 'cause she's not fighting me.

That sassy mouth of hers is closed, and her legs are spread just enough for me to get her off. I chuckle in the crook of her neck.

My stubborn peach is at least willing to put her guard down long enough to let me get her off. Maybe she's thinking she'll just get off and leave me hanging, and to be honest, I'm fine with that. For now.

Her chest rises and falls with her heavy breathing and she licks her lips as I slip my fingers past her panties and circle her clit. My dick is hard as steel as I feel how hot and wet she is. Damn, she's good at putting on a front and denying herself what she wants.

I watch as her eyes go half-lidded and her lips part.

What I wouldn't give to be able to bite that lip right now.

I circle her clit and nip her earlobe as she whimpers. "Quiet," I whisper into her ear.

She tries to keep her expression neutral, but her eyes close as my fingers dip into her hot, wet cunt.

Fuck, she's going to feel so fucking good on my dick. I pump my fingers in and out, stroking her G-spot and press my palm to her clit.

I'm so fucking hard, I'm leaking precum.

I gotta get her off and try to get Katie outta here, cause I *need* to be inside her.

I feel it the moment she cums. It's fucking perfect.

Her pussy clamps around my fingers and her body trembles. She shoves her ass into my dick and I can't help but to rock a bit into that thick ass so she knows how much I want her.

An explosion on screen muffles her small gasp. She throws her head back and I catch her lips with mine.

It's fucking perfect.

And then I see Katie get up and tiptoe her way out of the room from the corner of my eye.

Chapter 11

Madeline

Explosions jolt my body, and it's hard not to cry out as I throw my head back. Zane's thick fingers continue to bang my pussy even as I spasm around his fingers and press my ass against his big dick. My breathing quickens, my vision blurs and the room spins as pleasure becomes my existence.

I don't know how much time passes before I come back to earth, but when I do, Katie is mysteriously gone from the room and Zane is staring at me with a big satisfied grin on his face.

Wow. I can't believe I just let him do that, I think with shock, falling out of Zane's lap and shuddering. But it felt good. Incredibly good. And I want more. But how could I let this happen in the first place?

It's Katie's fault, I blame. *She was supposed to keep this from happening.*

I search for her in a panic and find she's nowhere around. Shit! Did she see? Or did she leave before things got so heavy? Was it her way of giving Zane permission to have his way with me? I bet she fucking did. Whatever it was, she's gonna pay dearly for her treachery.

Damn you, Katie!

I decide to take my anger out on Zane. "You asshole!" I snarl.

Zane looks bewildered. "Huh? Why are you mad at me, peaches? I was just trying to loosen you up."

Oh, you loosened me up alright, I think wryly, trying to keep my eyes level with his face. I'm painfully aware of the huge bulge in his pants and my juices all over his fingers.

"Our date is over." I stab a finger at the door. "Leave. Now." I'm not sure why I'm being this way. This man just gave me the best orgasm of my life and now I want him to get away from me before...

Zane doesn't budge. "C'mon. Our date can't be over, especially after that."

But *that* is the very reason our date should be over. Because I'm too fucking scared of what's coming next.

"Oh yeah? What do you think we should do then?" I don't give him a chance to answer and instead say accusingly, "I know exactly what you want to do."

Zane stares at me with a hunger that is palpable. "I ain't

gonna lie, peaches. I want that sweet, tight pussy of yours cumming all over my dick. Right now."

His words almost make me swoon. Seriously, the way he says things, he could open up his own phone sex line. And the bad thing about it is, I want exactly what he wants. Even though I just experienced an explosive orgasm, I'm ready for another one. So fucking ready.

"I've wanted you since the moment I laid eyes on you," he continues. "You're smart, sassy, sexy and very funny. And I haven't ever met a girl like you, so how can you blame me?"

I stare at him, fighting my raging hormones, fighting my emotions. With each passing second, I'm losing the battle. After just cumming all over his hand, it's hard to justify not giving in and letting him have his way with me. Fuck, I want him to use my body.

"Just give me one chance, peaches," he reasons, his voice dipping even lower than I thought possible. "To cherish you, worship you, and… be inside of you."

That's it. I can't take it. I want him to fuck me like he owns me. I want *him*.

I grab him by the hand and lead him upstairs. My heart pounds in my chest and my body heats with equal amounts of anxiety and desire. We fall back on my bed and he doesn't waste a moment to kiss me passionately. His hands roam all over my body as our tongues do battle, and I moan with need. Maybe I knew this was going to happen. I couldn't avoid it.

He wants me, and he's a man who always gets what he wants.

Before I know it, my dress is being ripped over my head and I find myself in just my bra and panties. Zane moves to remove my bra, but I stop him, my heart pounding in my chest.

"Wait," I gasp.

"What?" His eyes are burning with fiery intensity, his breathing ragged. He looks like a man that's run a mile and is thirsty as fuck.

I tremble beneath that hungry gaze. "I don't know if we should do this." How I'm still resisting by now, I have no idea.

Zane is having none of it, and begins undoing my bra, his eyes promising pleasures beyond my wildest dreams. "Come on peaches, let me show you what you're missing." He brings his lips forward and kisses me up my neck until he reaches my lips, which he devours, sucking and gently biting on them.

It's over. I'm fucking done.

As he lays me back on the bed and begins to take off my last pieces of clothing, dismantling my resistance bit by bit, I finally surrender myself to him. And somewhere, through all the moaning, I hear him whisper in my ear, "And you're going to fucking love it."

Chapter 12

Zane

I see her defenses fall down around her. I see the vulnerability in her eyes. Her lips part, and a soft moan escapes. Finally! I crawl toward her slowly and press my lips against hers. I'm not going to let her regret this.

I moan into her mouth, and slip my tongue in, massaging hers and enjoying her hands tangling in my hair. *Let go, peaches.*

She rocks her pussy against me and it's almost more than I can take.

I'm so fucking hard for her. She's all I've wanted for so long. I want this to last.

I gently pull her bra free of her arms. She shakes out her hair and tries to cover herself from me shyly.

"No you don't, peaches." I can see the hesitation in her eyes and the distrust. My girl doesn't like to be told what to do, but that's only because of another man doing her wrong. She'll learn to love what I do to her.

She'll learn to trust me. I'll show her.

"I wanna see you. I wanna see every inch of your beautiful skin."

I lean down and kiss her neck. She tilts her head, letting a soft moan of pleasure escape and exposing more of herself to me.

My fingers grip the edge of her panties and I'm slow to pull them down her thighs. I kiss my way down, loving the feel of her beneath me and the way she writhes from my touch. I plant kisses on her breasts, her sides, her hips. I look up at her and leave one on her clit.

She looks down at me with a vulnerability I'm growing to love.

I take a languid lick of her heat.

I groan and close my eyes. Peaches. "So fucking sweet." A beautiful blush colors her cheeks. I stare into her eyes as I suck her clit into my mouth and massage it with my tongue. She tries to keep my gaze, but her head falls back and her hands fly to my hair.

I suck harder and slip two fingers into her soaking pussy.

Fuck, she's so tight and hot. She's going to feel like heaven on my dick. I curl my fingers and stroke her G-spot, needing to get her off again so I can get inside her.

I *need* her.

I kick my pants off as she cums on my fingers. Her arousal leaks out of her pussy and I'm quick to lick it up. Her body jerks and trembles, and her eyes close tight as her release takes over.

I push my boxers down and cage her small body in under me.

I line the head of my dick up as the last of her orgasm flows through her. I dip into her pussy slowly, loving how tight and hot she is for me. I hold my breath as I push all the way in, making her back arch. Her nails dig into my back and her forehead pinches as she struggles to take all of me. I kiss the crook of her neck and give her a moment to get adjusted to my size.

She feels so fucking good. I knew she would. I groan against her neck. I knew she'd feel just like this.

I rock slowly and listen as her moans of slight pain become moans of intense pleasure. It doesn't take long until she's rocking her pussy and pushing me in deeper. Her heels dig into my ass, begging me for more. And I give it to her.

I don't hold back.

I thrust into her, holding her hips down so she forced to take all of me and everything I'm giving her.

Over and over I impale her with my dick. She screams out my name and it's the sexiest fucking sound I've ever heard.

I need to cum, but I don't want to yet. I don't want this

to be over.

I've finally gotten a taste of her. I've broken down a wall I'm not sure she'll leave down for me. I know there's a good chance that the moment this is over, she's going to regret it. And I don't want that. I can't stand the thought that she'd ever regret being with me.

I push harder into her. I pound into her tight little pussy with everything I have, holding back my need to cum.

Her neck arches, and she screams out as her body trembles beneath me. The urge to cum is strong, but I don't. I won't. I want more.

I need to give her more.

I cover her nipple with my mouth and suck, keeping up my ruthless pace.

Her body pushes against mine as she screams, "Zane!" Her scream is a plea. I know this is intense, but I'm going to give her everything I've got.

I pull back and release her nipple with a pop before doing the same to the other side. My blunt fingernails dig into her hips, holding her still as I pound away, taking pleasure from her, but giving her so much more.

"Cum for me, peaches," I whisper in her ear. And just like the good girl she is, she obeys.

The feel of her hot cunt pulsing around me is more than I can take. I erupt inside her, releasing wave after wave of hot streams. I cum harder than I ever have in my life.

I give her short, shallow pumps until I'm spent.

I look down at her, her eyes closed, mouth parted. Her skin is flushed with the most beautiful pink. She slowly opens her gorgeous green eyes and I can see everything in them.

She can't hide a thing from me.

I see her desire, her fear. I see her for who she really is.

And I want her.

I need her.

I refuse to let her regret this.

Chapter 13

Madeline

I hear the door creak open and I become slightly annoyed. I don't like being woken up before my alarm clock goes off. Katie should know that by now.

"Go away!" I growl at her from under the covers, pulling them tighter over my head and burying myself in the warmth of the bed. It's too comforting. I'm not getting up.

If Katie knows what's good for her, she'll leave me alone and go on a run by herself.

A soft smile slips into place as I hear the door close and I'm able to relax slightly. I prepare to drift peacefully back to sleep.

But then I hear a sexy chuckle that causes my pulse to quicken.

"You're not a morning girl, peaches?" Zane whispers.

I have to blink a few times and lower the covers, but only enough to see him.

Crap, I have no makeup on. I'm in an old baggy t-shirt... I look like shit.

And oh my god. Morning breath.

No, he cannot be here.

I totally kicked his ass out last night for this very reason.

I mean I was as nice as I could be, but I don't want to ruin this before it even starts because of my morning breath!

I open my mouth to tell him to get out, but he crawls on the bed toward me with a heated look in his eyes. The look of a predator.

I shake my head and sit up slowly, backing away from him.

He smirks, like it's cute.

"How the fuck did you get in here?" I ask him, just to change the subject from you-can't-fuck-my-brains-out-when-I-have-morning-breath to anything else.

He smiles, and I'll be damned if he doesn't look completely doable right now. He hasn't shaved, so he has a sexy bit of stubble I want to feel scratching on my inner thighs as he eats me out. His hair looks wild, and it's begging me to run my hands through it. But I still haven't even processed what happened last night. He left me exhausted and sated. I kicked him out, took a quick shower and crashed. Hard.

"Katie let me in."

"That bitch!" Fucking Katie is going to be my downfall.

He laughs at me and cocks a brow as he says, "I can see why she said good luck."

I bite my bottom lip and look down at the covers. What happened last night was amazing. I can't deny that. I can't deny how alive I felt under him. But I'm too scared to fall for him so quickly. It's not safe. And I know that's what's going to happen if I'm not careful. I can't let it happen.

I have to protect myself.

"Zane, I--"

"Shh," he puts a finger to my lips. "Don't think about it." My lips soften against his finger and he pulls away. "I just need you this morning." He leans forward for a kiss and I reluctantly give in. I can't deny I want him. I'm tired of fighting.

"Let me make you feel good."

I try to talk, I have every intention to object, but the soreness between my thighs reminds me of last night. My clit throbs as if I've been primed and ready for him since he left.

He pulls me down under him by my hips and I let out a small shriek.

He grins at me as he says, "You need to be quiet, peaches." He lifts my t-shirt up high enough to kiss my belly. "In case Katie comes back," he whispers against my pussy. His thumbs loop around my panties and with a quick tug, he shreds them into nothing.

My eyes go wide and my mouth opens into a perfect O

as he licks my clit and pushes two thick fingers inside of me. Yes! He feels so good.

My nipples harden and I remember pinching them for him. I remember how he came watching me. I quickly pull the t-shirt off and do it again. My fingers roll my hardened peaks and then I gently pull. There's a spike of pain that's hardwired to my clit and I fucking love it.

He taught me that. He gave that pleasure to me.

He looks up at me from between my legs with a hunger that makes my pussy clench around his fingers.

He groans, "Fuck, baby. I need to be inside you."

He sits up between my legs and moves his dick back and forth between my pussy lips, pushing in before I have a moment to even think.

Fuck, I barely think as my head falls back.

I hold in my breath as he pushes his rigid cock deeper and deeper.

The stinging pain of being stretched to my limit combined with the ache from last night makes it almost too much. But then his thumb rubs against my clit, and the delicious mix of pleasure and pain makes my body crave more.

He stills deep inside of me and kisses my neck, my jaw, my lips.

I arch my back and then tilt my hips. I need more of him. More.

As he thrusts his hips, I let out a strangled cry of pleasure.

My head thrashes, but he grips my chin and crushes his lips against mine.

I feel like I can't move; I don't even want to breathe.

I only want him.

He kisses me with a passion I thought I'd imagined last night.

I kiss him back with everything I have. No thought, only feeling. My body is moving on pure instinct. He devours my kisses like they were meant for him and him alone. My nails dig into his back, and I urge him on.

He pounds into me, taking more and more of me each time.

He pulls away and takes in a breath, pulling his shirt off. His muscles ripple, and the sight alone makes me clench around him.

He owns me in this moment. I know it. He knows it. He towers above me with power and lust. And I *love* it. I *want* it.

He doesn't ask, he merely flips me onto my knees and hammers into me from behind, taking me how he wants me. I can barely hold this position. My fingers dig into the mattress and I struggle to stay up as he fucks me ruthlessly. The wet sounds of him slamming into me again and again fill the room. I feel so weak and helpless, but more than that, deliciously used. And overwhelmed with a pleasure I've never felt before.

He leans down, pressing his chest to my back. His deft fingers find my clit and he rubs mercilessly.

Too much. Too much.

I bury my head in the pillow and he bites and sucks my

neck and back, alternating with kisses. All the while fucking me with a relentless pace. I arch my back and he goes in deeper. Fuck! I moan into the sheets, biting down on them to muffle my need to scream.

And just when I think it's too much, and I can't take anymore, we both cum violently.

A blinding white light flashes before my eyes, and paralyzing pleasure flows through me.

He kisses my spine all the way up to my neck. He grips my chin in his hand and kisses me like he needs me. My heart swells, and I find myself kissing him back passionately. In this kiss I'm not holding back, I'm kissing him with the same intensity he's giving me.

As my orgasm leaves me and reality sets in, fear begins to overwhelm me. I didn't want this. I don't want to be in a position to get hurt again. And that's just what he'll do. Like all men do. My breathing speeds up, and the only thing I can hear is my heart pounding in my chest.

"You have to go," I tell him as the tears threaten to reveal themselves.

I've fallen too hard, too fast. I'm only going to get hurt.

"You okay, peaches?" he asks. He asks because he cares. But that'll change. I know it will. And I'll be stupid enough to believe he really does care about me. I'll be the one getting hurt, and it'll be all my fault.

"I'm fine, but Katie's going to be back soon." I wipe my

eyes with my back turned to him. But he sees.

He grips my arm and makes me face him.

And I can tell by the way he tilts his head and gives me sad eyes, that he knows I'm going to lose it any second.

Chapter 14

Zane

Fuck, I don't know what happened, I don't know what I did. But she's already trying to run from me. I'm not gonna let her.

"Come here." I pull her into my arms without giving her an option to leave me.

As soon as she's in my arms, she starts crying.

"Did I hurt you?" I know it's a tight fit and I was a bit rough with her, but I thought she was loving it.

I finally got her underneath me, and I took it too far. Fuck! I've never hurt a woman like that before, but I lose control when I'm with her. I can't believe I hurt her. I feel like such a selfish prick.

She shakes her head in my chest, and I don't understand.

"Tell me what to do," I say as I sit back on the bed and pull her into my lap. Our cum leaks out of her and onto my leg, but I don't give a fuck. I'll clean her up later.

"I'm scared, Zane," she whispers so quietly I almost don't hear her say it.

I smile gently into her hair. My chest feels like a weight's lifted off of it. I didn't hurt her. She just thinks I'm going to.

She's too sweet. Too much of a good girl. But now she's my good girl. I'm going to make sure she knows it.

"You're scared I'm gonna hurt you?" I ask her.

"Yes," she heaves a breath and lifts her face away from me. Her cheeks are reddened and tearstained, but somehow she looks even more beautiful. Her vulnerability and raw emotion are things I find even more gorgeous. I fucking love that she's sharing with me. But she wasn't going to. She was going to push me away. That shit's not happening.

"I know how guys are," she says flatly. Huh? Where's all this coming from?

"What's that supposed to mean?" I ask her.

"Guys cheat--"

"Women cheat, too," I say as I cut her off. I'm nipping that shit right in the bud. I stare into her eyes, willing her to tell me what the fuck is going on in her head.

"Yeah, well, men are good at making up excuses for it and telling you that they love you and making pretty promises all the while thinking about fucking someone else." She's tense and on edge, and I get the feeling this isn't about me, and it's not about us. It's about something else.

I pull her closer to me and tell her truthfully, "Whatever asshole did that to you, didn't deserve you." Her eyes widen slightly and I add, "I'd never do that."

I take her chin between my fingers and make her look at me. I brush my lips gently against hers and rest my forehead on hers.

"Listen to me, Maddy," I start to tell her. My heart thumps in my chest with anxiety. I'm making her a promise in this moment. But I know she'll be the one to break it.

"I'm here, and I'm not going anywhere."

She opens her eyes slowly and looks at me like she's afraid to believe me.

"I'll be yours and only yours, if you'll be mine," I offer her.

She wipes her tears away and searches my face. My heart stalls in my chest as she seems to take forever.

"Don't leave me hanging, peaches. Haven't you done that enough?" I ask her with feigned desperation.

That gets a laugh from her. I fucking love that sound.

"Deal," she says simply with a small smile and a spark of happiness in her eyes.

"You wanna go somewhere later?" I ask her to change the subject.

"Where?" she asks with a little pep in her voice that wasn't there a moment ago.

"The parlor," I suggest. I've been wanting her to come see it. If I give her a little more of me, maybe she'll relax and just enjoy this. My eyes roam her naked body as she tries to cover herself with her bed sheet. I'm tempted to rip it out of her hands, but I let her cover herself. She needs it.

"You mean where you work?" she asks, and my eyes snap up to meet hers.

"Can we bring Katie?" Maddy asks. "She's been wanting to check out a tattoo parlor for some time now." I think that'll make her happy, and if it means she'll say yes, then fuck yeah Katie can come. She seems better when she's got Katie around her, more at ease.

"Sure. I don't see why not. It'll give Needles someone to talk to."

Maddy frowns. "Needles?"

"He's a friend." I'm trying to be casual about it all, but really I'm excited. This is my passion, and Needles is a good friend of mine. Really my only friend.

She seems a little giddy at the prospect of getting to see where I work.

"And maybe you'll agree to get a tattoo from me," I add.

Her eyes widen like I've lost my mind. "I don't know about that."

"Oh come on," I lean in and kiss her neck before whispering in her ear, "Tattoos are sexy."

She leans away and seems to consider it.

"What kind of a tattoo do you think I should get?" she asks and then purses her lips. I know she's the kind of chick who would detail out every curve of a tattoo before letting me put it on her. It's no fun for me, but that's just who she is.

"I have the perfect idea," I tell her.

She stares at me, waiting for me to continue.

I wink at her as I say, "Peaches."

She playfully slaps my arm and leans into me. It makes me feel good. Disaster averted. For now, anyway.

It's only a matter of time before she realizes how fucking bad I am for her. But I'll let her be the one to call this off. I'll let her walk away if it gets to be too much for her.

But until that day comes, I'm gonna enjoy her as much as I can.

She really is too good for me, and one day she'll realize it.

It fucking sucks, but I know it's going to end before I've had my fill of her.

Chapter 15

Zane

"Wow, this place is pretty rad," Katie quips, looking all around as I open the door for the girls to the tattoo parlor. I feel that Maddy needs to see where I work to be at ease. I know she has her doubts about me, and I need to show Maddy that she doesn't have any reason not to trust me. Hopefully this'll do it. Or help at the very least.

"It is," Maddy agrees. Even though I know tattoos aren't her thing, I can tell she's impressed with the layout of the shop. We have squeaky-clean checkered floors, a lot of goth artwork on the walls, and framed pictures of clients with our most impressive tattoos. Maddy walks around, leisurely looking at all this stuff before she finds her way over to the counter.

"So is this where you give tattoos?" she asks as she runs

her fingers over a photo album of our work.

"Yup," I respond. "I'll show you the back later, peaches," I say with a smirk at Maddy and give her a wink. In typical fashion she rolls her eyes, but I know she's dreaming about me fucking her on my table now. Fuck, I'd do it right now too if I could, but I don't want Katie to get the wrong idea about me. Right now she's on my side, and I wanna keep it that way.

Needles comes out of the back carrying some tattoo tubes in his hands. He's about to say something, but he stops when he sees us.

"Hello," Maddy says politely.

"Heya," Katie greets. She eyes Needles with curiosity, who's dressed in all black with his goth tattoos on display. I can tell that neither Katie nor Maddy are used to being around guys like Needles, and I wonder how this meeting is gonna go down.

Needles looks at them and then at me. "Who are these chicks?" he asks.

"Prostitutes," Katie says before I can respond. "The two dollar kind."

I chuckle. "These chicks are my girl, Maddy, and her friend Katie." I gesture at Katie and then add, "Ladies, this asshole is Needles." That gets a laugh from them and I expected the side-eye from Needles, but his eyes are focused on Katie.

"Oh, sup," Needles says. "Welcome to Inked Envy, where we hook you up with the best tattoos." He pauses then as if he just realizes something and looks at me with his forehead pinched. "Your girl? Since when did you get pussywhipped?"

"Since I broke up with your mom." I'm quick with a response, and I keep it light.

Katie snickers at my response, which I know she loves.

"Well that was bound to happen, considering mom's as loose as a sinkhole."

"God, show some respect, douche," I growl. Seriously, Needles is making me wanna fuck him up. He's a shit wingman.

"Sorry," Needles says without a hint of authenticity. He turns to Maddy. "It's just that Zane hasn't been in a relationship in... well... never."

"Is that a bad thing?" Maddy asks. She's side-eyeing me nervously, and I can only assume all sorts of dubious thoughts are running through that pretty little head of hers.

Needles walks over and sets the tubes down at his workstation. "I just don't see him settling down is all," he replies. "He's never been able to have a relationship that lasted more than a week.

Maddy grows quiet and I literally want to take Needles outside and curb stomp him. Does he have any idea that I'm trying to make Maddy feel comfortable with dating me? It's like he's going out of his way to shit all over my effort.

It's one of Needles' character flaws. He always speaks bluntly, even if it means offending someone. It's one of the reasons why he's my friend. He's real, not fake and phony like most of the people in my life. But right now his penchant for truth is annoying the fuck out of me. She doesn't need to know that shit.

An uncomfortable silence falls over the room, and I feel like I need to say something to put Maddy at ease, but I'm saved by Katie.

"One of you give me a tattoo!" Katie demands out of nowhere. "Right on my ass!"

"Katie!" Maddy protests. "I thought you hated tattoos."

"Not anymore."

"I'd be more than happy to if you're serious," Needle says, staring at Katie intently. He seems to have a thing for Katie, but I think she's out of his league. I'd give him less than an hour before he said something that would offend her and have her clawing him for blood.

"Well, I'm not," Katie admits.

"Damn," Needles says with disappointment. "That would've been the highlight of my week.

Katie blushes. "How'd you two even meet?" Maddy asks, looking between me and Needles. She seems quick to keep Katie and Needles from getting a little too close, and it makes me wanna laugh at her. They're grown ass adults. If they wanna have a go, let 'em.

I look at Needles with a grin.

"So he came into my shop one day. Not this one, but a different one."

Needles is turning red, and I can't help but crack up

laughing. "He got hammered one night and decided he'd give himself a tat."

I turn to Needles. "Show 'em."

Needles looks a bit pissed at me for even bringing it up. He's done all his tats himself, and he's good at what he does. But that night he shouldn't have done that shit.

"Nothing good happens after 2 a.m.," he says, lifting up his sleeve.

"Looks good to me," Katie says and shrugs her shoulders as she lets her fingertips graze Needles' skin. His lips turn up into a soft smile.

"That's 'cause he came to a pro to fix his shit work."

Needles' smile vanishes. "You were sober. That's the only difference."

I chuckle and wrap my arm around Maddy's waist, bringing her closer to me. She seems so much better now. So much happier.

"What about you and Katie?" I ask her.

Maddy looks with a scowl at Katie, who is grinning mischievously. "Don't. Just don't," she warns.

God, this is gonna be good. I can already tell from the look on my peach's face.

"Well, we're kinder buddies," Katie says.

"Kinder buddies?" I ask. My brow furrows, what the fuck is a kinder buddy?

"Yeah, we met in Kindergarten, so we're Kinder buddies.

We were so young though, I don't remember much."

Maddy seems to relax and trust that whatever Katie has on her, she's not gonna tell. But judging by the way Katie's smile just grew on her face, she's not gonna keep quiet

"Except this one time, where Maddy--" Maddy runs to Katie and gets a hand over her mouth, cutting her off, but Katie manages to pull away and dodges Maddy's next grab. They're on opposite sides of the counter now. Katie's got a huge ass grin on her face, but Maddy just looks pissed.

"It's not funny, Katie!" Maddy's shooting daggers at Katie, but Katie just keeps grinning and continues.

"She was on the playground," Katie begins. Maddy darts around the counter, but Katie's faster.

"And she fell from the top of the slide." They look like two kids playing as Maddy chases Katie around the counter, trying to catch her. "And I went to help her. 'Cause you know, I'm such a nice person and all."

I look at Needles, not believing this shit is really happening.

Maddy stops running, and the two try to catch their breaths. Maddy points her finger at Katie and says, "Just stop right now, and I'll never tell--"

Before Maddy can finish her threat, Katie spits out, "And she had completely soaked her clothes!" She starts laughing hysterically, and Needles follows suit. "She literally scared the piss out of herself."

"I was like four!" Maddy yells. She still looks pissed, but

more embarrassed than anything else. I wanna laugh, but I hold it in. Something tells me she'll never forgive me if I laugh at her for this right now. "I swear to God, I'm going to tell every story I can when you finally hold down a boyfriend," she mutters.

Needles stops laughing and looks at Maddy and says, "I mean, at least you were four. It could be worse."

I grunt out a laugh. "How old was that fucker that shit himself while you were giving him a tattoo?"

"Too fucking old!" he answers, and just like that Maddy relaxes a little.

"Oh. My. God. Are you for real?" Katie asks Needles with disbelief.

"I shit you not," Needles says, and I just shake my head, but it gets a laugh out of Katie.

"Oh my God!!" Maddy shrieks out of nowhere. I actually flinch. Grown ass men can't even make me flinch. "This is my song!" she yells out and takes my hand. I didn't even notice the music in the background. I generally just tune it out. It's more to help customers relax, not for us.

"What are you doing?" Needles asks as she pulls me in front of the counter.

"Dance with me!" she says. I stare into her beautiful green eyes, and I can't deny her.

"You're really fucking gonna dance!" Needles crows. He's having the time of his life with this shit.

I shoot him the finger behind Maddy's back as she sings

along to whatever song is playing.

Katie whips out her phone to take a picture. Fuck, not a picture. Probably a video judging by the fact she's still got the damn thing raised.

Normally I'd just sit down and refuse to do this shit. But looking down at Maddy, she's so fucking happy, just having a good time.

Whatever, I can sway back and forth and let her have the time of her life over a song.

I push her away for just a second and she looks up, thinking I'm done. But I've got her hand in mine and I go for the twirl. I figure if Katie's recording, I might as well do something to make it worthwhile. Seeing Maddy smile makes it worth it.

She busts out a laugh and so does our little audience.

My heart swells in my chest as she gives me a wide smile and leans into my embrace again.

And then, in a split second, all the happiness is gone when I see Vlad walk up to the building with a scowl on his face.

"Needles," I call out even though my eyes are on the door. "You wanna take the girls out back for a second?"

Maddy's forehead pinches and she looks at me like I owe her an explanation. But she sees where I'm looking and turns in my arms.

"Just head out back, baby." I plant a kiss on her nose. I'm trying to keep it casual and not let on to the fact I'm pissed he's here. I don't want her around this shit. And I don't want him to ever lay eyes on her. But it's too late.

Vlad bangs on the door with his fist. Since the shop is closed, the door is locked. He fucking knows that.

"I'll be out in a minute," I say and give Maddy a smile as she looks at Katie, and then to Needles. She looks uneasy, and I know I need to settle her down some.

"It's just business." That's not enough to get the nervous look off her face though. Vlad's a scary ass looking dude. "I promise after this I won't be working any more tonight." I speak with a relaxed, easy voice as Needles starts walking them back.

"Let me show you guys the equipment I have in my trunk." Both women stop dead in their tracks, and I shake my head on the way to the door. Dude has no fucking game.

"I mean, my stereo system," he says.

Katie cracks up and asks, "What year is this?" She's joking, but Needles doesn't laugh. He knows how serious this shit is.

I walk to the door and pull out my key, listening as they open and shut the back door. I open the door wide and move to the side to let him in. "Vlad, nice to see you." It isn't really, but what else are you gonna tell the mob boss?

I've never liked Vlad or the shit he does. If it wasn't for Nikolai, I'd never feel comfortable enough to stay anywhere around these fuckers.

When the head of the mob is a cold-blooded killer with a taste for women way too close to being underage, it's hard to feel safe. He's backstabbed more than a few people. But I've always felt like I was on the inside. I guess that's only because I know Nikolai would give me a heads-up. He said if you don't know who's on the hit list, then it's 'cause your ass is close to being on it.

Every move Vlad makes is calculated. I've never given him a reason to even think about me. I stay out of his way and just let them take over the books for their laundering.

"You throwing a fucking party in here?" Vlad sneers. His cruel blue eyes stare back at me. He's a tall blond man with combed-over, thinning hair.

"I'm just showing a couple of friends the place is all."

Vlad's glare says it all. His eyes seem to say, *'What the fuck is the matter with you?'*

"Get those bitches the fuck out of here. Now."

Everything in my body screams at me to tell Vlad to go fuck himself, and I would, if I didn't think he would do something to harm one of the girls in retaliation.

"Okay boss." I turn my back on him and go right to the back. At least he doesn't follow me back here. I don't need him around either Katie or Maddy.

"You guys have to go," I say as soon as the door shuts behind me. Katie's leaning into the trunk of Needles' car messing with one of the speakers.

"Why?" Maddy asks; she's got concern written all over her face.

"We were having so much fun," Katie whines in protest.

"Just take my car and head back home."

Maddy looks like she's going to argue as I pull her a few feet down the street to where I parked. I need to make sure she doesn't. When it comes to Vlad and all this shit, I need to make sure she listens to me.

"It's just business, peaches." I open the door to my car and hand her the keys. "I'll be back as soon as this meeting is over."

It hurts to see Maddy's unanswered questions in her eyes. She wants to know what's going on. But I can't tell her. No fucking way.

I can see her starting to question everything, and I fucking hate it. I wanna tell her. I want to make sure she trusts me. But I can't. The more she knows, the worse it'll be for her. That, and she'll leave my ass.

"I shouldn't have brought you here with the chance of my old partner coming by," I tell her. It's a mix of white lies. It's true that I didn't know he was showing up tonight. But "old partner"... well that's just a flat-out lie.

But it does the trick. Her lips purse and her shoulders relax some. "So you're just settling *old* business?" she asks with her arms crossed, and the keys tapping against her forearm.

"Yup. And it'll be over with soon. So I'll be right behind you." That part's true. At least it better be.

This is my shop and if I want my girl here, she can come here. I just need to make sure I keep her ass away when *business* is going down.

Chapter 16

Madeline

"So how's things with Zane?" Katie asks as we pull into our parking space in front of the condo. As we stop, I notice a car across the street that looks familiar, but I'm distracted and can't quite place it.

I glance over at Katie who's staring at me intently, hungry for juicy gossip. Dressed in a red tank top and white pants, her side bob is on point today and looks extra shiny underneath the bright sun. I have to admit, she looks cute. Too bad she hasn't been acting cute. For the past few days she's been pestering me with constant questions about Zane. How good is he in bed? Does he know how to work it? Did he have a monster dong? And so on and so on.

"Where they shouldn't be," I respond flatly.

Katie scowls, sensing my bitchiness. "What's that supposed to mean?"

"That I shouldn't have had sex with him, much less be talking to him."

"Oh, c'mon Maddy. Really? It can't be that bad. You've had a serious glow about you for the past few days."

"Seriously, thanks to you, I'm in this predicament." I know I shouldn't be doing this to Katie right now, but I'm about falling for Zane. Hard. When I'm with him, everything's great. And then I leave his side and doubt spreads through me. I just don't trust it. There's something off.

Katie eyes go large and her mouth opens so wide a giant trout could jump through it. "Me?!" she exclaims. "What the hell do I have to do with this?"

"You didn't protect me from Zane like you were supposed to," I accuse. She knows it, too.

"What the hell? What are you, two years old? I mean, what was I supposed to do, tell his big dick to stop wanting you?"

I roll my eyes. "You know I don't mean that--"

"Seriously Maddy, grow up. You need to have this experience with Zane. If nothing else than to teach you that not all guys are the same."

"That's the problem, he talks a good game, but in the end he's not any different from any other horndog out there."

Katie sighs, and places a comforting hand on my shoulder.

"Maddy, I understand how you feel, I really do, but that's not the way to live life. You're supposed to have these experiences, so that you can grow. Shit, I'd rather have lived and smoked cock every once in a while than to never have smoked cock at all."

As serious as I feel right now, I have to laugh. "Really, Katie? Smoked cock? That's a horrible analogy!" Leave it to Katie to say some ridiculous crap to pull me out of a bad mood.

Katie scowls at me. "I never said I was good at it. I'm just trying to get you to cheer up and see reason."

"I know, Katie, I know. And I'm sorry about blaming you for what's happened. It's not your fault. I wanted this just as much as Zane. Maybe even more. I'm just feeling really scared right now and I guess I'm just freaking out."

Katie smiles at me. "Well, I'm glad you see that. And I think you should stop worrying. Now. Sit back, relax, and let this all play out. If Zane doesn't wind up being a good guy, you know what? Fuck him. Trust me, there are many more big dicks out there in the sea."

I giggle. I'm already feeling somewhat better. "Oh Katie, what would I ever do without you?"

"Probably never laugh and be a sourpuss all the time."

"Ain't that the truth," I agree, chuckling.

We gather our books, get out of the car and go into the condo. As soon as Katie swings open the door, my jaw drops at the sight before me.

"Daddy?" I ask in shock. "What are you doing here?"

There, standing in the middle of the living room, is my father, Kenneth Murphy. At sixty, his hair is white as snow, but that's his only visible sign of aging. He has a smooth, unlined face and crystal clear blue eyes. If not for the hair, he could easily be mistaken for a man half his age.

He's wearing black slacks and a white dress shirt with a tie, just a little too formal for a retired parole officer. There's a bulge on the side of his dress shirt letting me know he's carrying. Daddy never leaves the house without his gun. Ever. Now I know why the car outside looked so familiar. He could have flown, but knowing Daddy, he decided to drive so he could make a nice vacation out of this visit.

The bigger question though, is how the hell did he get inside of our condo?

"Well, hello Mr. Murphy!" Katie greets my father before he can respond, walking over to him and giving him a big hug. "Boy, do you get more handsome each time I see you, or what?"

Daddy chuckles at Katie's shameless flirting. "Thanks, Katie. It's nice seeing you, too. How's school been treating ya?"

"Oh you know, a little bit of that here, and a little bit of that there. I think I'd go crazy if it weren't for Maddy."

Daddy's eyes twinkle. He's always been one to play along. "So you two been getting along well, I take it?"

Katie nods. "Uh huh, except--"

I cringe, bracing myself for Katie to blurt out something stupid about me and Zane.

"She farts so loud when I'm trying to sleep."

My father lets out a goofy laugh and I roll my eyes while loudly protesting, "Katie!"

"I'm just kidding." She points at the hallway. "I'm gonna go take a shower and let you two play catch-up. It was nice seeing you again, Mr. Murphy."

"It was nice seeing you too, Katie."

When she's gone I ask, "How the heck did you get in here?"

Daddy walks over and sits down on the couch. "You two left the door unlocked. I figured after the door swung ajar when I knocked I'd better sit here until you two arrived back home."

How the hell was the door unlocked? I could've sworn I locked it when we left.

"You really should always lock your door," Daddy says with a disapproving frown. "There's all sorts of sick predators out there, waiting to prey on young, vulnerable women like you both. Have I not taught you that?" As part of law enforcement, my father was big on safety growing up, and he never failed to lecture me when he thought I was being careless with my welfare.

"We do lock the door," I object, trying to fight back irritation. I hate being scolded. But I know my father is only saying these things because he cares about me. "I just don't know why it wasn't locked today. That's all."

"Well you can't afford to not know, Maddy. One mistake can cost you your life."

I sigh in exasperation. "Daddy, I know--" He cuts me off before I can finish speaking.

"Do you always carry that can of mace with you like you promised me you would?" he demands.

I look down guiltily at my bookbag. "No," I reluctantly admit. "But I'm going to start doing it, I promise."

Daddy shakes his head and stares me in the eyes with disbelief. "Damn it Maddy, it won't do you any good sitting at home!"

I'm taken aback by the venom in Daddy's voice and tears begin to well up in my eyes. I feel sick to my stomach. I hate making my father unhappy and disappointing him. "I'm sorry," I choke out. My father never yells at me like that over something stupid. "I haven't been able to think..." my voice trails away as the image of a cocky, smiling Zane pops into my head.

Suddenly repentant, Daddy pats the seat next to him on the couch. "I'm sorry baby, come sit down over here. I didn't mean to yell at you."

Pushing back my tears, I drop my bookbag and go over to him. Damn, I'm just so emotional lately. With Zane and the stress from school, every little thing is getting to me. As soon as I'm there, he envelops me in his arms and kisses me hard on the forehead. "Will you forgive me?" he asks.

"Of course," I say. "I know you're just upset because you

worry so much about me." He's a cop, and ever since mom died, all he does is worry about me.

Daddy nods. "Yes, I do." After a moment, he leans back to study my face intently. "Is something else bothering you, or are you still upset with me?"

"Huh?" I ask, astonished at daddy's unerring observation. I shouldn't be surprised, though. Daddy's an expert at reading body language, and he probably sensed there was something wrong with me the moment I walked through the door.

Daddy gives me a knowing look. "Don't play stupid with me, Maddy, I know when something is on your mind."

I bite my lower lip and think. My father will know if I'm lying if I try to play it off. I don't want to tell him though. Daddy's overprotective as it is, and I already know he's going to hate Zane. I can imagine his disapproving stare already.

"Maddy?" he persists.

He's not going to stop until I tell him.

I let out a big sigh and admit, "I'm seeing someone."

My father's instantly back on edge. "Who?"

Taking a deep breath, I tell Daddy everything, holding nothing back. He's been my voice of reason my entire life, and I can't lie to him. I don't want to. I even admit to my father that I'm falling for Zane. I don't know why, but I'm always able to confide in Daddy.

When I'm done I feel relieved. It's almost therapeutic, telling my father about my feelings, worries and doubts.

"So let me get this straight," Daddy says slowly, "You met this fellow and you think he's a player, yet you still slept with him?"

Cringing, I nod.

He asks disdainfully, "And he's a tattoo artist?"

I nod again. Fuck, I should not have done that. Regret consumes me as my body heats.

Daddy stares at me, his eyes boring into me so hard I can sense the anger behind them.

"What?" I ask, flinching at what's to come.

"Jesus, Maddy, a tattoo artist?" he snarls. "What the hell is wrong with you?'

"Daddy, I--" Again he cuts me off.

"Do you think I sent you off to school just to get involved with trash? You're supposed to be looking to go places in life. Not hanging around with some trashy, deadbeat womanizer."

Anger twists my stomach. "He's not a deadbeat," I say hotly. "Nor is he trashy. And he obviously supports himself well enough as an 'artist' since he has own place."

Daddy snorts with derision. "He might be peddling coke on the side, for all you know. You've already said you don't even know if he has other girlfriends, so what reasons do you have to trust this guy?"

As much as I hate to admit it, Daddy's right. What did I know about Zane before I slept with him, except that he was sexy as all hell and a tattoo artist? I know nothing of his past, don't even know how many sexual partners he's had. And with what happened at the shop with his *old* business partner, I'm beginning to have serious doubts.

Daddy's features soften. "I don't mean to be an asshole to you, Maddy," he says, sensing my inner turmoil. "I just care about your well-being. And I would prefer you not get mixed up with someone who obviously isn't a good fit for you. You need to let this fellow go so you can focus on your studies."

For a moment, I begin to seriously regret telling my father about my business. I have this sneaking suspicion he's going to start suddenly showing up on my doorstep unannounced just to check on me.

While I appreciate his concern, I won't be able to handle that. Whether or not Zane is bad for me, I don't need someone else dictating what I should do in this situation. As Katie said, I need these experiences to grow and mature.

"I know where you're coming from, Daddy, really I do," I say softly, but then I harden my tone and add, "But I'm fine. You shouldn't worry about me. Whatever happens between me and Zane is my business."

Daddy stares at me for a long moment, but I hold my ground. I feel like he wants to tell me that I'm forbidden to see Zane and that he's going to move me to another condo, but at the same time he's conflicted by the fact that I'm an adult who can now make her own decisions.

"Are you sure about this?" he asks finally, grudgingly.

"Yes," I reply, visibly relaxing. "Don't worry, if I do need you, I'll call you."

"Promise?"

I smile. "I promise."

I feel a sense of relief. We got through this discussion without my father demanding to see Zane so he could threaten him to stay away from me. Now all I need to do is to convince him that I don't need him to check up on me every day, and I'll be more than fine.

I open my mouth to ask my father about what's been going on his life instead of focusing on me, when the doorbell rings.

Right then, two words run through my mind along with a feeling of dread.

Oh no.

Chapter 17

Zane

The door opens, and all I can think is, *fuck this shit*. A white-haired man dressed in black slacks, a dress shirt and tie stares back at me, and I watch his eyes as they take me in. Narrowing, judging. Yeah, I've seen this before.

I'm a beast, and I look the part.

I usually don't give a fuck, but my girl is standing by the stairs looking nervous as hell. My heartbeat picks up. My nerves buzz with an insecurity I'm not used to feeling.

I know this isn't going to last. We're just enjoying each other for now.

Shit, when she's done with school, she's gonna leave me far behind. I know it. I've accepted it. But I just got a taste of her. I'm not ready for this to end now.

"You must be Maddy's father," I say as I reach my hand out to the old man. "Nice to meet you, sir." He lets it hover there for a moment, a moment that lets me know what he really thinks. Finally he takes it in his with a firm shake.

"You must be Zane." His voice is hard and unforgiving. "Maddy's told me about you."

I nod. "Yep. Zane Stone." I say this clear and proud. Although shit, I wish I'd known he was here.

Maddy clears her throat, and I can practically hear her heart pounding.

Maddy takes a few steps toward us and pushes him out of the doorframe so she can take my hand in hers. My heart swells in my chest.

"Daddy, as I was telling you, Zane is my..." she hesitates to finish, but looks right into her father's eyes with squared shoulders.

I've never been anyone's *boyfriend* before. But for her, right now, sure. I can be her boyfriend. "Boyfriend," I say the word with my eyes on her, but clear my throat and look up at her father.

He's fucking pissed.

It means a lot that she's willing to stand by me as her father clearly dislikes my existence, but I don't need to stay around for this shit.

I just came by to fuck you. I can't say that. But shit, it's the truth. I was looking forward to it too. "I just came by to see how your test went." She's been on and on about this damn test lately. But I'm sure she aced it 'cause she's a smart girl. And that sounds a fuckton better than her dad hearing me describe all the ways I wanted to relieve her from all that stress.

She pulls me into the foyer and I resist, but she whips her head around and tugs harder. Her father stares at our hands and I wish I could just fucking leave. Fine. For her, I'll put up with this. Only because she stood by me. And that felt so fucking good. She'll never know.

I walk with the two of them to the dining room. Maddy's books are open on the other end, with her notebook out and highlighter.

She takes a seat at the other end and pats a seat for me. This ordering me around shit isn't my forte. But I'll let her take the lead on this. After all, it's her father. And I'm sure I'll get brownie points if he likes me.

I take the seat next to her and look up at the old man. Fuck, there's no fucking way he's gonna like me.

He's looking at me like... well, like I'm fucking his daughter. I can't help the grin that grows on my face.

I lean forward and give Maddy a smile. "How'd it go?" I ask her.

I can feel his eyes on me, but I ignore him. I usually don't take this shit. If a fucker's gonna give me a look like he's got something to say, I don't stand down till that shit is dealt with. But this is her father, I've gotta show some respect.

He gets this one moment. One day. That's it.

Maddy takes a deep breath and pulls her hair back. "Well, I think it went *okay*."

Before she can say anything else, her father interrupts. "So your real legal name is Zane?" he asks.

I turn to him and sit straight in my seat. "That's right, Zane Michael Stone." I don't like how he's looking at me.

"That's an interesting name." He says the words in a monotone, his eyes boring into my face. Also, what the fuck does that even mean? An interesting name?

I shrug my shoulders and say, "I didn't pick it." Maddy huffs a small laugh, but it's forced. The tension in the room is thick, and this is uncomfortable as hell.

"So, Maddy," he says as he looks at her like I'm not even in the room with them. "You didn't say Zane was a smartass."

I keep my mouth closed and let him have that one. Point one for Pops, I guess.

"Daddy, please don't do this now." Maddy's lips are pressed into a thin line and she's staring back at her father like she's ready to tear him apart.

Fuck, maybe I'm lucky not to have my parents around anymore.

Her father looks back at me, but before he can speak, Maddy tries to lighten the mood by saying, "So, I think we should all go out to eat. We could go to a nice restaurant," she suggests. She looks at me and says, "Besides, you owe me a date. And this way Daddy could get to know you." She sounds slightly hopeful and upbeat. I take a look at Papa Fuckoff, and I know that's not happening. My stubborn peach is apparently also delusional.

"I just don't get it. What do you see in him, Maddy?" he asks, leaning close to her with his elbows on the table.

I drop Maddy's hand and clench my fists under the table.

"Daddy," Maddy's tone takes on a hard edge. I'm not sure what the protocol for this shit is. I've never been in this position before.

"She's seen a lot of me, to be honest; she must've liked at least one part," I say with a straight face.

He looks fucking furious. I can't really blame him, but I'm not gonna let him talk to her like that. After a minute he shakes his head at Maddy like he's disappointed in her and that's the last straw, but before I can say anything, Maddy lays in on her father.

"Daddy, I love you," Maddy says as her eyebrows raise, and I can see she's holding back that inner bitch she's unleashed on me a time or two. "But you need to stop this. Now."

I stare at my stubborn little peach who's all full of sass today. But this isn't the same shit she gives me. This is different. She's not playing a game, she's clearly upset, and I don't like it.

"Hey, it's alright." I take her hand in mine and rub

soothing circles on the back of her hand with my thumb. "It's fine." I'm partially amazed at how well trying to calm Maddy down diffuses my own temper. So what if he doesn't like me? He's not the first. And I'm sure he won't be the last.

She doesn't need to get worked up over this. I mean, isn't a dad supposed to hate the prick who's doing his daughter? Pretty sure this is all normal. And her father's right. I don't look like the kind of man who she'd normally pick. Not that she picked me. I had to fucking fight for her.

My heart sinks a little, and I hate all these bullshit emotions that are hitting me. I need to get the fuck out of here.

I stand up from the table and give Maddy a small smile as she grips onto my arm. "I should give you two some time, peaches." I let her nickname slip, and see her father stiffen on my left.

"Nice to meet you, Mr. Murphy." I say it as a formality and don't look him in the eyes as the words come out hard.

"You don't have to go," Maddy says in a soft voice with her forehead creased. I bend down and give her a chaste kiss.

"I get to see you every day." I look back at her dad and give him a curt nod as I say, "You should spend some time with your father."

"I'll walk you out," Maddy says and tries to get up, but I stop her.

"Nah, I'm only next door, I can find my place myself." I have to repress my laugh as her father starts coughing.

Maddy's mouth presses into a thin line and she gives me a look. I can't help the smile growing on my face.

"Talk to you later, peaches," I say and give her another kiss goodbye.

"Have a nice stay, Mr. Murphy." I give him a wave as I open the door and walk out.

Chapter 18

Madeline

I spend the next five minutes scolding my father for his rude behavior toward Zane. Just because I have reservations about him, doesn't mean it gives Daddy leeway to be a total jerk to him and judge him like that.

Daddy argues with me, telling me he doesn't like what he saw in Zane, and that I don't need to be messing around with him. Through it all, I hold firm. Despite my misgivings, I'm not leaving Zane without good reason, and that's final.

Eventually, Daddy gives up, but he does warn me, much to my chagrin, that he'll be watching.

As soon as my father's gone, I decide I need to go next door and apologize to Zane for Daddy's behavior. I feel anxious and embarrassed by what's happened, and want to make amends.

I walk over to Zane's and knock on the door. After a moment, the door swings open and my jaw nearly drops.

Zane's standing there in a pair of pajama bottoms hanging low, balanced precariously on his chiseled hips, that incredibly sexy V-shape at his lower abdomen fully on display. Down below, his large cock presses against the flimsy material, making my mouth water.

Good God, this man is beyond sexy! I think to myself.

Seriously, I want to fall to my knees and take that big fat cock out and start slurping on it like a straw jammed into my favorite milkshake. It's a nice distraction, but I can't help how my heart is squeezing in my chest.

I forcefully tear my eyes away from his bulge and ask, "Are we okay?"

For a moment, Zane stares at me and my heart begins to pound with anxiety, but then he cracks that boyish smile of his. "More than okay, peaches." He reaches out, grabs me by the waist and pulls me into him. I melt into his body. Lower, I feel his cock pressing into me and I'm immediately turned on.

I'm so turned on that if he wants to fuck right here in this doorway for all the world to see, I won't have any objections.

Zane must have plans though because suddenly he pulls me inside, closes the door, and hefts me up onto his shoulders. I cry out with surprise, my legs trembling. "What are you doing?" I demand.

"We're better than okay," he says as he pulls my dress up and pushes his thumbs through my panties, ripping them off of me. Oh fuck. That's the sexiest thing I've ever seen. I push my head back against the wall and grip onto his hair as he licks my pussy. Holy fuck. He's not wasting any time.

He says something about me being a good girl before dipping his tongue into my pussy. "Uhh!" I lean forward involuntarily as my legs tremble around him.

"Zane!" I call out, trying to balance myself. His blunt fingernails dig into my ass, forcing my pussy to rock against his mouth. Holy fuck, it feels so good. My toes tingle and a low stirring of pleasure builds in my core. My back goes straight and my legs go stiff as he sucks my clit into his mouth, and then dives back to my entrance. Fuck, fuck, fuck.

I'm going to cum. It's the fastest I've cum in my entire life.

My breathing comes in short pants.

I rock my pussy against his face and grip his hair tighter, shoving him deeper. I'm so close. My nipples harden, and I want so badly for his dick to be inside me. I need him. My head rocks to the side. So close. He pulls away and I almost curse at him for leaving me on edge, but he quickly shoves two fingers inside and massages my clit with his tongue. Fuck yes! His fingers mercilessly stroke my G-spot and he bites down lightly on my clit. Oh shit! YES!!

My back bows, and I let out a strangled cry.

"Fuck!" I scream out as he eats me out like he's starving and my release crashes through me. My pussy clenches around his tongue, and he groans as I feel the pool of arousal leak down my thighs. My cheeks heat with embarrassment, but I feel so fucking good I'm not sure I care all that much. He keeps lapping at my pussy until I'm limp.

He gently sets me down on shaky legs. I lean against the wall and catch my breath.

"My peach is juicy," he says with a smirk as he wipes my cum from his face. I feel that heat in my cheeks again and try to right myself.

I'm out of breath and shocked, and I don't know what to say. Shit, maybe he should meet the rest of my family. I wonder what he'd do if he met Grandma.

"Come on, I want to take you somewhere," Zane says to me after our explosive oral session. I'm barely over my orgasm, my legs still trembling. It's amazing what Zane can do with his mouth and those powerful jaws.

Just remembering the way he suctioned my pussy makes me want to experience it again... and again... and again.

"Where?" I ask, feeling completely off-balance.

"A date," he says simply. "You're delicious and all, but I gotta eat a bit more tonight."

I rock nervously on my heels, feeling stupid for even asking after *that*. "So we're good? My Daddy--"

Zane puts a finger over my lips. "We're good, peaches," he

says and starts to say something else, and I can feel my heart beating faster. *I love you.* I know that's what he was going to say, but instead his mouth slams shut.

I feel a tinge of disappointment, but I shove it down.

I bite my lip, debating on saying it first. But no, that's not fucking happening. I pull up my bra strap and then pull my dress down.

"Dinner it is." I give him a small smile and I can tell he's waiting on me to say more. But he's not getting it.

If he thinks I'm going to be the first to say I love you, he's wrong about that. Just as soon as the smug thought comes to mind, I realize maybe he wasn't going to say that.

Insecurity sweeps through me. Fuck. When did I let this happen? I love him. The realization hits me hard, but it's true. It just happened so naturally with all the time we've been spending together lately that I wasn't even aware of it until now. I'm in love with Zane... but he's a bad boy. I'm sure he doesn't love me. Guys like him don't fall in love.

It's only a matter of time before he leaves me.

"Let's go, peaches." He wraps his arms around me and I do my best to forget my father's advice screaming in my head and ignore the painful insecurities telling me I need to end this before he breaks my heart.

He plants a kiss on my cheek and opens the door.

I know he's bad for me, and this is really going to hurt when he ends it. I won't tell him I love him, but I'm done pushing him away.

I may not say it out loud, but I fucking love him. How the hell did I let that happen?

Chapter 19

Zane

"You're so bad," I whisper into Maddy's ear as we leave my workroom.

I lock it behind me like I do every day after my shift. But today we're leaving a little early.

She's been coming here every day to hang out while I work. It's our little routine. She goes to school, then comes here on Tuesdays and Thursdays. She's got all-day classes the other days of the week, which is perfect with my schedule. So on those days I meet her at her place later on, and fuck up her good study habits.

"We're gonna be so late now." Maddy's freaking out.

"Well you're the one who bent over in that short ass dress."

That'll teach her to wear something like that out. Actually, knowing my girl she'll probably wear them more often now. I smirk at her as she tries to fix her hair in the mirror behind the counter.

"You look good, babe." She does. She looks sexy as fuck. "How'd I get so damn lucky?" I wrap my arms around her waist and pull her toward me. I yank her up enough that her feet come off the ground and I bury my head in the crook of her neck.

"Stop!" she yells at me with a smile on her face while she's pushing off of me. I chuckle at her. I don't think she'll ever stop pushing me away.

"We gotta go," she says and grabs my hand the second I put her down. She starts pulling me toward the back exit where she's been parking.

I'm so caught up in how happy she makes me, I don't think about what day it is, or what time it is. I just let her lead me to the back.

As soon as she pushes the doors open and I see the van, I pull her back in, but it's too late. Four men are moving a pile of coke bricks onto a cart to take inside.

Fuck!

"What the--" she starts to ask, but I pull her to me and turn on my heels with her in my arms. My body heats with anxiety, and then I look up and see Garret walking out of the stockroom. I'm quick to pull Maddy to my side and walk past him.

"Whoa, where are you two headed?" he asks the two of us, but his eyes are on Maddy. She shifts on her feet and puts her body behind mine. I can tell she's not okay. She finally put two and two together.

My stomach drops, and I feel like shit. I feel like I lied to her, even though I didn't really. It was a lie of omission. Worse than that though, I put her in harm's way. Real fucking danger.

I'll do everything I can to keep her safe, but the way Garret's eyeing her is making me want to put a bullet in his head right now.

"Heading out," I answer him flatly. I know I look pissed. I can't help it. I can't school my features and play this off like she didn't see shit.

He gives me a crooked grin and nods. "See anything you like out there?" he asks Maddy.

She shakes her head, but doesn't give a verbal response. Her fingers dig into my skin, begging me not to let her go.

"See you later, Garret," I say and pull her to my other side. We walk straight out to my car. We'll come back for hers later. Right now we just need to get the fuck away from here.

I can't think. I don't know what to do.

This shit isn't good.

Witnesses don't live to be witnesses. I know that much. I know Garret's gonna tell Vlad, and then I'm fucked. I need to call Nikolai. But first I need to fix this shit between us.

I pull the passenger door open and gently push Maddy

into her seat. I know she's still fucked up because she's not talking. She's chewing on her thumbnail and looking all around her. Shit, she doesn't even look like she's breathing.

I reverse and pull out without saying anything. The silence stretches between us for way too fucking long.

I need to say something, do something to make this right. But I don't know how. This just drives home the fact that I'm all wrong for her. I'm trouble, just like she said I was.

"You alright?" I finally ask her. I can't look at her though. My hand grips the steering wheel tighter as I slow to a stop at a red light. My heart beats frantically and my lungs won't fill. But none of it matters, because she's not looking at me. She's not saying shit.

Her walls are up, and she's looking out the window as silent tears fall down her cheek.

Fuck! I can't stand this. The light turns green and I step on the gas to get us home.

A lump grows in my throat and it stays there until I park the car.

She's quick to unbuckle her seatbelt and try to get out, but I don't let her. She tries to smack me away, but I'm not letting her leave like this.

I pull her into my lap and let her beat her fists on my chest. A sob rips up her throat. Her face is red and her cheeks tearstained. She's fighting my hold on her, and I take it.

I take it all. I fucking deserve it.

When she finally seems to give up and collapse into me, I tell her, "I'm sorry, peaches." I don't know what else to say.

"You--" she tries to speak as she wipes under her eyes, but she can't. Her gorgeous green eyes stare out the window as she tries to calm herself.

"I'm sorry," I tell her again, but I know apologies don't mean anything to her.

"You deal drugs?" she asks with an accusatory tone. She doesn't look at me. She's staring at her condo.

"No. The mob does." That gets her attention. She faces me with her brows raised in both fear and surprise. Her voice goes up an octave as she says, "You're in the mob!"

I shake my head and say, "It's not like that."

She shakes her head and hunches her shoulders, wrapping her arms around herself. "I need to go."

I grip her hips, I can't lose her. I know if I let her go right now, she's gone forever. But it needs to happen. Fuck, as the realization hits me, my chest seems to collapse with pain.

"Peaches, don't--"

"Don't call me that!" she yells at me, and looks at me with a raw sadness I've never seen on her face. I hate it. I hate what I've done to her.

"I'm sorry, Maddy."

Her composure breaks, and I can tell she's holding back more tears.

"I'm sorry. Just, just tell me that you won't say shit."

That's all I need from her, and I'll let her leave me.

She looks at me with fear in her eyes. "I didn't see anything."

"Good girl." I try to kiss her, but she pulls away from me. I should expect that.

"I'm sorry, Maddy." I know this is the end. But I don't want it to be over. "Is this it?" I ask her, hating how I'm leaving it in her hands.

Her body shudders with a sob, and she falls limp against me.

"I don't know," she answers with her head buried in my chest, and I hate it. I hate that she's making me be the one to pull the trigger. We need to be over and done with though. I can't let this shit I'm in get to her.

I'll make sure no one comes after her. I'll call Nikolai. I'll get this dealt with. I knew I was going to be bad for her. I never should've let it get this far.

"I'm sorry, Maddy. I'll leave you alone now."

She cries harder against me. But only for a moment.

"Fuck you, Zane." She pushes against me and opens the driver's door, climbing out. She angrily wipes the tears away and walks to her door with her arms crossed over her chest. I sit in the car way longer than I should. Wanting to chase her, but knowing I shouldn't.

Chapter 20

Madeline

I walk up the stairs, each step feeling heavier than the last, my breathing labored. I'm feeling an array of emotions; anger, sadness and rage. Unspeakable rage. I want to hit someone, preferably Zane.

I knew it! I rage, holding on to the anger and ignoring the pain in my chest. *I knew he was no good for me. Why did I have to be so stupid?*

I tried to fight him. I can't deny I knew this was bad. I brush the tears away and hold on to the railing as I slowly walk up the stairs.

He's a drug dealer! I want to scream, but if I open my mouth, I know I'll just cry. *A fucking drug dealer!* A shudder runs through my body. That man was no good. My heart freezes remembering the way he looked at me. I nearly fall on the step remembering the man from a few weeks ago. Fuck! The signs were there. I'm so stupid. He lied to me! How could he?

If my father only knew. He'd be fucking furious. He all but warned me not to trust Zane, but even with my misgivings, I went along with the bad boy anyway. How stupid am I? How stupid could I have been to not see what was in front of me this whole time?

I make it up the stairs and to the window of my bedroom. I peer out and see Zane's car still parked by the sidewalk. He's sitting there, staring straight ahead. A part of me wants to run back out there and scream at him, accuse him of lying to me, but another part of me just wants to remain away from him. Far away. It doesn't matter what I do though. No matter what, I'll be hurt. And if I run to him, he'll only hold me and try to make me feel better. And then what will I do? When I'm in his arms, I'm a fucking idiot. I'm weak and stupid when I'm with him. I slam the curtain closed and turn my back on him. I put my hand over my mouth and try to stop crying. It just hurts so much.

My bedroom door opens and my heart stops, thinking it's Zane.

"Maddy?" Katie asks with astonishment. "Maddy, what's wrong with you?" She's quick to run to my side and I lose all composure.

I collapse in her arms, sobbing like a baby. "Zane," I wail. I try to tell her what happened. About the drugs, the man, the breakup. I try, but even I can't understand my words.

"Huh?" Katie asks in bewilderment. "Maddy, stop crying, you're babbling and not making sense."

It takes great effort to get a hold of myself. I sit up, wipe at my teary eyes and focus on Katie. She's looking at me with shock, probably wondering what the hell is going on. "It's Zane," I manage to choke out over a sob.

"Zane? What did he do? Cheat on you?" Katie scowls darkly. "If he hurt you in any way Maddy, I swear to God, I'll twist his dick until it's curved."

"No, he didn't cheat," I say and gulp back another sob. "At least I don't think so." But he's a fucking liar. *What else did he lie about?* Even as I think the nasty thought, I know it's not true.

"Then what? What did he do that was so bad that you're in here acting like a maniac?"

"He's a drug dealer. Or at least he deals with people that deal drugs." It's the second one. It has to be the second one. I refuse to believe he's any more involved than just owning the place. A million ideas run through my head.

Katie's jaw drops. "A drug dealer? Are you serious?" she squeaks.

Sniffling, I nod. "I saw these guys unloading pounds of coke at his shop."

"Holy shit!" Katie exclaims. She pauses and then asks,

"Are you absolutely sure?"

"Yes! I don't know what's going on, but I'm sure they're using the parlor as a front." I rub my eyes. They feel swollen and tired. I feel exhausted. And most of all, broken.

Katie shakes her head. "I can't believe it. He even brought us by there and let us meet Needles."

"I know, right?" I sniffle and try to hold on to that anger. "What a fucking fraud." I give her a pleading look. "What do I do, Katie?"

Katie takes a long time to respond, but she finally says, "The only thing you can do. Stay away from Zane. Far, far away."

Chapter 21

Zane

I wanted so fucking bad to go after her. I watched her close the door to her condo and I stared at it for a long time. I could've begged her to take me back. But what could I promise her?

I can't leave the mob. They'd hunt me down. They'd hunt *us* down. Marky's there now at my condo, keeping an eye on her house for me. I refused to leave until I had eyes on her. I called him the second I had the strength to get my ass back here and confront Garret.

I have a sick feeling in my gut. I may be overreacting, but I'd rather that than risk her safety.

It can't have been more than an hour since we left, but

the shop's deserted. I walk to Trisha's room, but it's locked. Needles' is open though.

"Yo," I call into his room, holding onto the jamb of the door. "When did they leave?" I need to know. Once they pick the shipment up it takes a few hours to drop it off. But then they'll be free to do whatever. I was hoping I'd catch them and make sure Garret stays away and leaves her the fuck alone.

Needles looks up at me from his drawing pad and opens his mouth to answer, but then his expression changes and he stands up, letting the pad fall to the floor with a dull thud.

"Bro, what's wrong?" he asks me and I back up, running my hands down my face.

I keep telling myself it's alright. I keeping thinking she'll be fine.

But I can't fucking lie anymore.

This shit isn't right. I'm not alright.

My heart twists in my chest. *She's* not alright.

"Maddy," I start to tell him, but my throat closes. I shake my head and pound my fist into the wall.

"How long?" I ask him again. My words come out harder than they should.

"Like fifteen minutes." I nod my head and swallow thickly. "What happened?" he asks again, and I know I need to tell him.

"I gotta call Nikolai," I tell him as chills run down my arms.

Fuck, having to make this call makes it that much more real.

I pull my phone from my pocket and dial his number. I shouldn't. I shouldn't be calling to talk about this shit. It's against code. Nothing is ever discussed on the phone. It's the reason I drove here.

I press the buttons and put the phone to my ear. Every ring makes me worry more and more, like he's avoiding me. Like maybe they're gonna take a hit out on me and keep me in the dark about it.

It's Nikolai, I tell myself. He wouldn't do that to me. He was everything to me growing up. He's not gonna fuck me over like that. Right?

Finally, he answers, "Yeah?" Hearing his voice answer the same way he always does is a good sign. A good fucking sign.

"Nikolai, I got a problem." I pinch the bridge of my nose and close my eyes. Fuck! I wish this weren't real. I wish I could just take it back. I'd take it all back to save her.

"You need me?" I can hear him move the phone and I'm guessing he took it off speaker.

"You don't know?" I ask him.

"Know what?"

"Something happened today at the shop."

"How bad?" he asks.

I shake my head and reply, "Not bad. It's just, my girl." I swallow thickly before continuing. "She was here and went out the back when the van was here."

"That's not good, Zane." Nikolai's voice is low. There's a

pause before he asks, "Did she see anything?"

I can't lie to him. "She saw a bit, but she knows not to say shit." I say the last words with conviction. "She's not gonna say shit to anyone." I start pacing the room with my hands in my hair. Needles is watching me like he's ready to go to war with me. He's always been a loyal friend like that. But he's nervous as fuck. "She's good for it. I'd put my life on it."

"Just calm down, Zane." He's talking like there's nothing wrong with what happened.

"I think Garret's gonna want her," I say, and I have to pause. I can't finish the sentence. I shouldn't, first of all. This is all going down on the phone and I can't say shit like that. But that's not the reason I can't get it out. The thought of them going after her makes me physically sick, almost unable to speak.

"We won't touch her. *He* won't touch her." He's quick to answer, and his words are absolute.

"I have a bad feeling, Nikolai." I'm telling him the truth. I really do. Something in my gut is telling me she's not okay, that she's still in danger.

"It's me, I got your back, Zane." Hearing Nikolai's voice telling me it's alright calms me down a good bit. Maybe it's all just in my head because I had to end it with her. Maybe that's why I feel so fucked.

I did need to end it though. She can't be around this shit. I'll never be able to bring a good girl into this shit life. I should've known better.

"She's a good girl, Nik," I tell him simply.

He chuckles low and rough on the other end. "I'm sure she is, and she's fine."

"Do you need anything from me?" I ask him. I can't imagine it's that easy. That she saw some shit, but they're just gonna let her go.

"Nah, it's all good." It's silent for a moment. "You alright?" he asks.

No. I'm not alright.

"Yeah, I'm good." I nod my head and look out the small window in Needles' room. "If it's all good and she's safe," I feel the need to clarify so he knows exactly what I'm saying. "Then I'm good."

He hesitates on the other end and my heart stops in my chest. But finally he responds, "It's all good. And I give you my word that she's safe. Go calm your ass down."

I wait another moment, letting the words sink in before I end the call.

"What'd he say?" Needles asks. I shove the phone back in my pocket and try to calm down.

"He said she's good... It's all good."

We stare at each other, neither of us saying shit, but I'm sure we're both thinking the same thing. *He's lying. She's a witness, and that means she's dead.*

"Needles, help me take her car back, man." I can't even look him in the eyes.

"Yeah, sure," he says as he takes a hesitant step toward me. "It's gonna be alright." He nods his head weakly, barely keeping eye contact with me.

Even he doesn't believe it.

Chapter 22

Madeline

I *shouldn't be here.*

It's been days since I last saw Zane. Yet, he's been on my mind ever since. Every waking moment has been spent thinking about him. I can't get him out of my head. The more I think about my situation, the more I begin to rationalize. So what if he's mixed up in a world of crime? Does that make him a bad person? He said he didn't sell them. That it wasn't like that. Maybe they pressured him. Maybe *he's* the victim.

I raise my hand and pause right before I knock on Zane's door, thinking, *I should leave.*

But I can't. All I can think about is Zane. I want to see him again, that cocky smile, that hot chiseled body. I want to feel his strong hands again, touching me, feeling me, caressing me.

I wanna feel better, and I know he can make me feel good. I know he can. He's like a drug made just for me.

Taking a deep breath and gathering my courage, I knock. There's no answer. I knock several more times. My knuckles rap against the wood and each time the hollow sound makes my heart squeeze harder and harder in my chest. Still no answer. I stand there for what seems like eternity before finally giving up.

He's not coming to the door. Bastard.

Feeling tears well up in my eyes, I turn away and walk back over to my condo.

It's a good thing he didn't answer, I tell myself as I storm back inside feeling mad as hell. *I should stay away. I always thought he was bad for me, but now I know for absolute sure.*

As much as I want to believe those words, I can't stop thinking about him. Maybe right now he needs me. God, I wish this ache in my chest would go away. I wish we could get lost in each other and just run away. I think about how well we went together, when the world would disappear around us. How much I miss his touch, his hot lips, his naughty words spoken in my ear.

Goddamn it, Maddy! Be strong!

But I can't. Just thinking about Zane makes me weak.

"Are you okay, Maddy?" Katie asks with concern as I brush

by her.

I ignore her and continue on to my room. There's nothing she can say that will make me feel better, and in a way, I blame her for my misery. After all, wasn't she the one that encouraged me to see Zane?

Katie follows me down the hall and up the stairs, but I pretend she isn't there. When I reach my room, I close the door on her. Before I can lock it, she pushes her way in.

I turn my face to the side to hide the tears. "Please, just go away!"

Kate walks in and closes the door. She crosses her arms across her chest and defiantly says, "No, Maddy. I refuse. I'm not going to let you walk around and treat me this way."

"I'm not treating you in any way," I deny.

"Bullshit. You're taking what happened with Zane out on me."

"No I'm not." My words sound hollow. Empty.

"Keep telling yourself that." Katie pauses and then accuses, "I saw you go over there."

"So what?" I reply defensively. "I wanted to talk to him."

"What the hell are you thinking? I told you to stay away from him." She's angry, and her words are like venom.

"You know that's funny, Katie, when you're the same one that encouraged me to give him a chance."

"Yeah, I did. I'm not ashamed of it either. How was I supposed to know he was involved in that shit?" I want to argue with her, but I bite my tongue. She's right. I can't blame her for not knowing the truth about Zane.

"You weren't," I admit grudgingly.

"Okay then. Now that I know the truth, I want you to do me a favor. Don't see him. *Ever.*"

My heart twists in my throat. It hurts. It hurts just thinking about it.

Seeing my tormented expression, Katie presses on, saying, "He lied to you."

"He didn't really," I find myself saying, "He just kept the truth from me. Which isn't exactly the same thing as lying."

I can't believe I'm defending him, I think to myself. *After all I've said about guys being no-good dogs, and now I'm taking up for someone who's been dishonest to my face.*

"Maybe I can change him," I say, trying to convince Katie as much as I'm trying to convince myself. "Maybe he'll stop."

"Are you even listening to yourself?" Katie asks with disbelief. "Is the same Maddy I grew up with, or did aliens abduct her and stick me with this clone? 'Cause you can't be serious."

"I know it sounds stupid, Katie, but... maybe Zane will change for me... I mean, I feel like he would..." I trail off weakly.

Kate raises a finger sharply, cutting me off from whatever I might say next. "Stop it, Maddy, just fucking stop. You tried this very thing with Zach. And did that work?"

"No," I admit reluctantly. Katie's right. It's just that I hate how I feel inside. I hate how I feel my very existence depends upon being with Zane. Being with him is intoxicating beyond words. Being without him is like being in a dark, lifeless abyss. "I just don't know what to do."

"It'll take a while, but get back involved in your studies and try your best to stop thinking about Zane. I'll even do whatever it takes to help you keep your mind off him. After a while, it'll be easy."

Katie's being overly optimistic. The guy lives next door and we're stuck in our lease for at least another year. How the hell am I going to stop thinking about him when I can look through my bedroom window and he's right there?

"You'll find someone else somewhere along the line in the future, someone who loves you and that'll treat you right."

I can't take it. I break down and start sobbing. I feel Katie's arms wrap around me a second later.

"Shh," she coos. "Everything's going to be alright." She comforts me. It feels good to be held. I just feel so damn alone without him.

When I finally stop sobbing she says, "C'mon girl. Pull yourself together. We got class in the next thirty minutes. That jerk-off is not about to ruin you like Zach did. Just be happy that you found out what you did before the relationship went any further."

After Katie's sure I'm okay, we take off to school. When we arrive, I'm a cauldron of bubbling emotions I can hardly contain.

I don't know why I agreed to come to class today, I think to myself as Katie pulls in between two trucks on the west side of the parking lot. *I'm a total mess.*

Katie gathers her books and begins to get out, but pauses when she sees I'm not budging. "What are you doing?"

"Sitting here," I say, trying to hold back tears.

Katie frowns. "Aren't you going to get out?"

"In a minute."

Katie opens her mouth to protest but I sharply say, "Katie, not now. Please. I need a moment to collect myself."

Katie stares at me long and hard. "Fine," she says reluctantly. "But don't stay in here too long. You'll just be making it worse." She climbs out of the car. Before she shuts the door she adds, "I'll be sending you a text to check on you. Answer it. And I'm taking the keys."

Then she walks off and I watch her for a moment before breaking down into tears. Luckily, this crying fit only lasts a few minutes, and after a few sobs, I'm able to pull myself together.

One day it'll stop hurting. I know it will. I just need to live through the pain and it'll go away. One day.

I gather my books and then check my makeup in the mirror. My mascara is all runny and smudged. I quickly fix it and then step out of the car. I'm about to round the car when I hear the sound of running footsteps.

Before I can turn around, rough powerful hands clamp down on my mouth. I try to scream, but there's a rag pressed to my face. I try to shake the hands off of me. I inhale deeply, and then belatedly realize I need to hold my breath. The rag is obviously laced with something to knock me out. Fuck! I struggle against the man. Or is it men? But my body feels weak. I'm losing control of my limbs.

Then I go unconscious.

Chapter 23

Madeline

I come to with my hair in my face. When I try to push it out of the way, I realize that my arms are pinned behind my back. I groan. I feel sore all over. Slowly, I open my eyes and experience a jolt of shock.

This can't be happening.

Though I'm bent forward with my hair in my face, I'm able to distinguish my surroundings. I'm in a chair, in a dark room and it's very quiet. Panicking, I struggle against my bonds, my fingers grazing against the rough material. Rope. Fuck! They tied me up. I pull harder, but I only succeed in burning my skin. It's tied too tightly. *Damn it!* Tears flood my eyes. Nausea twists my stomach.

Please tell me this is all just a dream.

But it's real. Very fucking real.

My mind is rushing with all sorts of doomsday thoughts. Who kidnapped me? Why was I kidnapped? And worse of all, what do they plan on doing with me? The latter thought terrifies me and chills my body.

Is it because of Zane?

I don't want to believe it. Zane wouldn't do something like this to me... would he? It's a scary thought. If it's true, it means I never really knew him all along. I try not to despair.

"Vlad, I have a gift for you," a deep, familiar voice says, startling me. Up until that moment, I thought I was alone. I turn my head slightly to get a visual on who's talking. My blood goes cold when I see who it is. Standing in a darkened corner is Garret with a phone pressed to his ear. He's staring at me in a way that makes me want to writhe against my bonds and get the fuck out of here, but the fear is so strong that I'm paralyzed.

"What do you think, boss, eh?" Garret asks on the phone. "She's older than what you're used to, but she's just your type." Garret laughs and then adds darkly, "The fighting kind." He smiles, a sick and disgusting sight that turns my stomach.

I can hear a voice on the other end and then silence, but Garret doesn't respond and keeps staring at me with those dead, chilly eyes.

I go dizzy with terror. "Zane!" I yell, tears streaming

down my face. "Zane, please don't let them hurt me!" I shake violently in my chair, struggling in vain to break free.

Garret's handsome face twists with rage and he walks over and backhands me in the face. I gasp with pain as my head whips to the side, and he snarls, "Shut up, you stupid bitch! That piece of shit ain't coming to save your ass."

The taste of metallic blood fills my mouth as stinging pain shoots through my face. Fuck, that hurt.

"Thanks to you, he's good as fucking dead." My heart stops beating. No. No!

Garret gives me a wicked smile at the look of confused distress on my face. "Yeah that's right, bitch. Zane is dead because of you."

"I-I-I didn't do anything for Zane to deserve this," I stammer. "Please don't hurt him.

"Lying whore!" Garret backhands me again and I cry out with pain. Hot fluid pours out of my nose. Blood. "You saw us unloading the coke. Ain't no way we're gonna let you live after that."

"I won't tell anyone!" I try to yell, but my mouth hurts so fucking bad. The small cuts sting, and I spit up blood. "I swear," I say weakly as tears prick my eyes.

Garret chuckles evilly. "No amount of begging or lying is gonna save you, cunt. If you didn't want to end up like this, you should've never got involved with that faggot Zane."

I start sobbing incoherently. This isn't fair. Not for me.

Not for Zane. Not for anyone.

I feel a hand touch my shoulder, and my heart nearly stops. *Oh no. Oh God, no.*

Garret chuckles at my terror, guessing my worry. "Don't worry, bitch. We're not going to rape you... yet. I gotta wait for the boss and the camera so we can give Zane a nice parting gift." His fingers touch my chin and I rip my head away. He smiles down at me as he says, "I want him to be able to watch."

"Fuck you!" I scream at the top of my lungs, no longer caring about what happens to me. At this point, I feel like I have nothing to lose. They're not going to spare me, and I'm not going to give him the pleasure of seeing me beg for my life.

Garret laughs at my rage. "We'll see how much shit you'll be able to talk when I have my dick in your mouth."

I sneer. "Fucking try it, and I'll bite your dick off."

"Fucking cocky bitch!" Roaring with rage, Garret shoves me and my chair topples over backward. My head slams against the floor, and I see stars. Through the pain I smile, pleased I made the evil fucker mad.

Garret lets out a snarl of frustration. "I can't wait to fuck you, bitch," he growls from somewhere above me. "You won't be talking shit after I get done. You'll be begging me to end your life."

As defiant as I've become in this predicament, I don't offer a response because I'm filled with terror.

When it's obvious I have nothing else to say, he mutters

something I can't hear and leaves. I hear the sounds of footsteps, followed by a door closing. I'm left alone with my thoughts and the knowledge that I only have minutes or possibly even hours left to live.

Please God, help me! I plead within the depths of my mind. *Please don't let my life end in this way!*

But God is either deaf or not listening. The truth is, no one is coming to save me. Not Katie. Not Daddy, and definitely not Zane.

I feel like there's only one thing left to do.

I close my eyes and pray for the end to come swiftly.

Chapter 24

Zane

My chest hurts so fucking bad. It hasn't stopped hurting since she came to my house the other day. I had to ignore her while she knocked on my door, but hearing her crying was like a knife to my heart. I wanna talk to her. I wanna explain everything. More than that, I wanna leave this life behind and take her away. But we'd have to run. We'd always be running.

You can't leave the mob.

Fuck, I can't handle it. But it's for her own good. I know it is. I've been keeping an eye on her. Marky has, too. I can't be around her all the time, and I trust him. He'd tell me if there was anything going on.

I can't sleep. Every time I hear a car pull up, I instantly think it's someone coming to take her. I've dialed up Nikolai's number at least a dozen times, but I never hit send. I need to know she's gonna be alright, and she's not on their list.

He told me she's alright. I have to believe him. I trust him.

But at the same time, I don't.

And Marky's still watching her when I can't. Just in case.

As if reading my mind, not ten minutes later I get a call. I stop working on the mock-up of the tat I'm doing later and calmly pick up my phone.

I'm trying to keep the worrying down to a minimum. Every time he calls my heart rate picks up, and dread runs down my spine. But each time it's always been to tell me she's fine.

I answer it and try keep my voice even, but before I can ask him about her, he's yelling on the other end.

"They got her." My blood runs cold. "I wasn't sure, Zane. I didn't want to freak you out." He's talking rapid-fire, practically shouting, and it's hard to hear. I stand up and pace the room as my body goes numb with fear. "I didn't know what to do so I just watched, but it was them and they took her. I tried--"

"Stop. Stop." It can't be true. My lungs refuse to fill. "Who has her?"

"Garret. That fucker and two others. I wasn't sure if it was him. It wasn't till I was pulling in and they got out. I wasn't fast enough. I followed them as fast as I could, but I lost them."

My blood races with adrenaline, anger takes over the fear. I'm gonna kill him. I'm gonna slice his fucking throat open.

"Where?" I ask him as I try to keep my hand from tightening on the phone to the point where it feels like it's going to break.

"I followed them onto Washington and then they went past"

"Where?!" I scream into the phone. I'm barely able to breathe, my vision's going white. I need to get there now. Right fucking now. Every second away from her is a second he could hurt her. Fuck, my heart sinks. He's going to. I know he is.

"I lost them going north on Market Street." Market Street? What the fuck is on Market Street? I don't know. I don't know shit about the mob's operations. Fuck!

I hang up the phone and immediately dial Nikolai. I'll fucking kill him. I'll kill all of them.

He answers the phone, and I don't give him a second to give me his bullshit.

"You lying motherfucker," I seethe into the phone.

"Whoa!" he yells on the other end, but I don't stop. I'll never stop.

"You told me she was safe. You're fucking dead."

"Zane!" he yells out.

"All of you are dead." I'll start at the top and work my way down.

"Zane! Who has her?" I pause in my oath to make all

them suffer. I wasn't expecting him to deny it. "Who has her?" he asks again, but I don't answer. I don't know if he's bullshitting me. My body's shaking with anger, and I'm not sure what to do. I don't know if I believe him. I don't know what to believe anymore.

"It's not us, Zane! I didn't lie to you. Zane!" He's quiet for a second. "Zane! Are you there?" He sounds panicked, and his voice is filled with concern.

"You didn't know?" I ask him while trying to calm myself down. A shred of relief goes through me. But only a shred. This will be easier if it's just Garret. So much easier if I have Nikolai's backing.

"It's not us--"

I cut him off. "Garret took her."

He's quiet for a second. I let it sink in, but in my head I hear the *tick tick tick* of time passing.

"Are you sure?" he asks.

"Yes," I'm quick to answer.

"Do you know where?" he asks. My phone beeps, and I'm sure it's Marky calling back. I pull the phone away from my ear and see I'm right. I ignore the call.

"They went down Market, but that's where we lost them."

"Give me her cell. They're probably at the warehouse." I rattle off her number and pace the room, feeling like a caged beast.

"What's the address?" I ask him. That's all I need. Just the address, and I can go.

"Hold on Zane, we need to know who's there."

"We'll find out when we get there."

"It only takes a minute, hold the fuck on," he scolds me, and I can't stand it. I need to move; I need to go to her.

"Fuck!" he yells into the phone, and it stops me in my tracks.

"What? What?" I ask him. Fear runs through me. Not Maddy. Please, fuck, don't be about Maddy.

"Vlad's there." His voice is hard and devoid of emotion.

"Vlad and Garret?" I ask him. My head feels dizzy and I have to lean against the wall. Pain tears through my heart.

"He's fucking dead." Nikolai's voice is cold. I nod my head at his words.

"How many others?" I ask him. He's tracking their cells to locate them. I've seen him do it before. Thank fuck for Nikolai keeping me from going in with no plan.

"I only see four of them. But there could be more."

"Do you have anyone?" I ask him. I can't ask Needles or Marky to come with me. They aren't trained for this shit. They wouldn't know what to do.

"Yeah, I do, but you need a vest, Zane." I don't fucking want to wait on a vest. "We have the element of surprise on our side. They won't see us coming. But we need to be smart." I don't care about being smart or being prepared, I just need to get to her.

"If I ever meant anything to you, you'll help me keep her safe."

"Zane, I'm on your side." He sighs into the phone and

says, "We'll get her back. I promise you."

My throat closes as other emotions take over, but I hold on to the anger. I picture what I'm gonna do to them when I get there. They're dead. Every fucking one of them.

"Garret's mine."

"You need to be smart about this, Zane," I hear Nikolai speaking, but I'm not listening. We're close, so close to getting her back and keeping her safe.

"You can't go in there guns blazing," he says. The fuck I can't.

"Nik," I say as I look him square in his eyes, "If you think I can go in there and not put a bullet in every one of their skulls, you've lost your mind."

"That's fine by me," he replies as he keeps my gaze, "But we need to go in quietly."

My jaw clenches. "I don't like it." He wants me to sneak in and find her. He wants me to wait for his call. I'm not fucking waiting. If they're in there... if they're with her. My throat closes and my fists clench at the thought. "I'll fucking kill them!" I slam my fist on the dash.

Nik looks at me like he's not sure what to do. "If it was up to me, Zane, you wouldn't be going in," he says quietly. "And you don't have to like it. But you need to respect my plan. I promised you we'd get her back, and I fully intend to keep that promise."

I bite my tongue as he continues. "You need to be quiet. You can't let them know we're there." He's right. Logically I know that. But logic can go fuck itself right now for all I care.

I hold his eyes and nod once. "Done." I'm lying. I'm not holding back. I refuse to stand by and watch and wait.

Nik looks behind me and asks, "Lev, Alec, you two loaded?"

"Damn right, boss," Alec answers. Lev nods. I look behind me at the two men. I've seen them before--hell, I've grown up with them. But I don't trust them. I don't trust any of them. I barely trust Nikolai.

For all I know, this is a setup and they're going to stab Nik in the back.

I'm going in and grabbing my girl, and getting the fuck out. If I can kill those fuckers who took her on my way out, that's what I'll do. She's all that's important. I need to get her out of there.

"We'll head in through the back," Nik says and starts giving orders. We're parked in a lot just behind the warehouse. He said there's no cameras here. I'm taking his lead, but I don't like waiting. I need to make sure she's safe.

Nik looks at me while he talks. "This hotheaded fuck is staying with me." He turns back to look at the other men while my eyes bore into his skull.

"You two need to make sure the place is secure. Sweep the place and kill anyone in there. Every single one of those fuckers is a traitor." They nod and agree, and with that I'm moving out of the car and I don't stop until we're there, staring at the steel double doors to the warehouse.

Nik is slow as fuck compared to me, but he's quiet. The other men are also quiet. All I can hear is my heavy breathing, and the sound of blood rushing in my ears.

I move to open the door, but Nik stops me. His hand flies to the handle and he rips my hand away.

Nik puts his finger against his lips and stares me in the eyes.

I nod my head and back away, following his lead. My heart's beating so fast and loud. I can feel it pounding against my chest.

As soon as I'm in, I hear her. The warehouse is nearly empty. To our right, I can see half a dozen folding tables with boxes piled high in two rows in front of them.

This must be where they pack and ship the product.

In an instant my head whips to the left.

I can hear her muffled cries for help. They echo off the wall. I move straight back, to the left. There's one hallway on this side, and her voice is easy to follow.

Keep screaming. I need to hear you, peaches. I need to know which door. My feet move of their own accord, and I'm only half-aware of Nik moving behind me.

I hear her cries from the far door, and I'm on it instantly. I'm there. She's still alive. I'm here. I can save her.

I go to grab the door handle, but Nik pulls me back. My

fists clench and I almost knock him out. But his attention isn't on me. It's on the door.

My shoulders heave as I wait for him to get going. I hear her scream out, and it's too much.

Nik's hand settles on the doorknob, gently turning it. I resist the urge to kick it open. I need to get to her. Her cries are louder now, and I don't know what's happening to her. My hands grip my gun and sweat pours down my face. My heart's beating too fast.

Maddy. I'm here.

Nik gently and soundlessly pushes the door open enough for us to creep through. As soon as I'm in, I see her in front of a desk, on the ground tied to an overturned chair. Vlad's standing above her with a large knife in hand. There's plastic wrap and duct tape on the desk. Their *equipment*.

Maddy's struggling against the ropes, trying to pull her hands free as she bucks off the ground. She's helpless and trying to scream through a gag. Tears are running down her face. My heart pangs in my chest.

Vlad's got a sick smile on his sunken-in face as he cuts her leg with the knife. Behind him, Garret's setting up a video camera.

Sickness threatens to take over, but more than that, anger. How dare they touch her? My body trembles with barely contained rage. Those sick fucks!

I can't let him touch her. I won't. In the distance, I hear gunshots. Alec and Lev must have found other people in the warehouse. But now we've lost the element of surprise as Vlad and Garret look up and realize we've come for Maddy.

I hear Nik yell as I run out to the middle of the room, my gun pointed at Vlad and firing. My hand's shaking so hard, I miss. The bullet sounds off and barely grazes Vlad's back. Garret comes from my left and throws a chair at me. The fuckers aren't armed.

Good. I aim my gun at him as the chair flies through the air.

It hits my calves and trips me up as I try to run to Maddy. I try to cover her, but I fall and the gun slips from my hands. It lands on the ground with a loud clank next to me, and I brace myself. I'm quick to get up and move to her side.

At the same time, I hear another bullet go off and see Nik go after Vlad from the corner of my eye. Garret's quick to run into Nik, knocking the two of them to the ground. Vlad's focused on Nik, and I can tell Nik is his target. I reach up to the desk and grab the knife.

Maddy first. I have to save her. Before I do anything else, I need her to be safe. I need to give her a fighting chance at least. I crawl to her and quickly cut the rope from her wrists. The knife saws back and forth.

I hear the sound of bones crunching and fists slamming into flesh. By the noises echoing off the walls of the small room, I know Nik must be putting up a hell of a fight.

Finally, the rope breaks and I hear Nik call out for me.

"Zane!"

I put the knife in her hands, knowing she needs to cut the rope on her ankles. "Run, Maddy!" I yell at her. "Run!"

I grab the gun on the floor next to me and turn to aim, but I can't fire. I could hit Nikolai. I move quickly through the room, kicking the chair and aim as soon as I have Garret lined up. He lifts his head and sees as I pull the trigger. He ducks and kicks off the ground, shoving his weight forward and pushing his body into my thighs.

I fall hard and the gun goes off as I crash to the floor. My hand hits the floor hard and I wince as Garret punches me in the gut. The gun slips from my hand and he reaches for it. I grab his waist and yank him down and away from it. He kicks my thigh and reaches for the gun again, practically climbing up my body. I headbutt his stomach, and he keels over in pain. I slam a fist in his jaw and it sends him sliding away from me, away from the gun.

I reach for the gun. I can feel the barrel with the tips of my fingers.

I see Maddy using the knife to cut the rope around her ankles from the corner of my eye. I need to kill him. I can't let him get to her. I need to get the gun first.

Maddy's screaming, and keeps looking at me. She needs to get out. Just save herself. But she's not running. She hurls her body at Garret with the knife in her hand. But he's too quick. He kicks her hard in her face, sending her flying backward.

Fuck! "Just run Maddy!" I scream to her, but she ignores me. I'll never forgive myself if something happens to her.

The knife slices his leg, but doesn't do anything more than slow him down for a moment. It's a moment I'm able to scoot closer to the gun than he is though.

Garret grabs my leg and tries to pull me away. I kick him. Hard. I miss, but on the way down my foot hits his jaw and he slips off of me. I kick against the ground watching Garret, and look up to see Maddy crawling on the floor and pushing the gun to me. I take it in both hands and roll onto my back, steadying it down my body and just as Garrett looks up, I shoot.

Bang! Maddy shrieks. *Bang! Bang!* I keep shooting until the gun's out of bullets.

Garret falls to the ground lifeless, but the fight's not over. I turn to my left and see Nik and Vlad both grappling on the ground, both with their hands at each other's throat. I aim my gun and fire, but it's empty. Fuck! My body's hot and my heart feels like it's racing to climb up my throat.

I search for another gun, but I can't see one. There's nothing.

I watch as Vlad puts all his weight on top of Nik and tightens his hands around his throat. Nik doesn't let up, but he's losing the fight. I can see it happening.

I run toward them and slam my body against Vlad's. He falls, and his hands slip. Nik takes in a heavy breath, coughing as his lungs fill for the first time since Vlad started choking him. I struggle to get up as Nik pushes against me and tries to pin Vlad's heavy weight down.

Nikolai's hands wrap around Vlad's throat. Vlad tries bringing his legs up to pin Nikolai to the ground, but I'm quick to grab him. I leave Maddy behind me and grip onto his calves. I push all my weight down and pin him. I don't let up until I see Vlad's hands move from Nik's throat to the hands strangling him.

The blood vessels in his eyes pop and his face turns red. Maddy screams. She doesn't stop screaming. I leave Nik and scoot backward to hold Maddy. She's on the ground, knife in her hand with the cut rope on the floor next to her.

Her clothes are torn, and the cut on her leg is bleeding pretty bad. I grab her in my arms and push my hand against her cut to stop the blood from flowing. I try shushing her. Her body shakes in my arms.

"I've got you. You're safe." I try petting her hair, but she's pushing me away.

My eyes focus on Alec and Lev as they come into the room with their guns out. I start to push her behind me, but they take in the scene and lower their weapons.

I hold Maddy closer to me as I see the life drain from Vlad's eyes. Lev walks over and holds a gun out to Nik as Vlad's body goes limp.

I turn Maddy's head away and watch as Nik puts the gun to Vlad's head and pulls the trigger.

Bang! Maddy jolts once in my arms, but she doesn't scream.

A clean shot in the skull. Blood spills from the wound as the head turns slightly and Nik moves off his chest.

"It's over, peaches. It's alright," I whisper into her hair, but she doesn't respond. That's when I notice she's not holding on to me anymore. She's limp in my arms.

"Maddy?" I give her body a firm shake as my heart races with panic. She's breathing, she's alive. But she's not responsive.

Chapter 25

Zane

She won't stop shaking. I hold her closer to me. I think she's in shock. "It's alright peaches, I've got you." I repeat the words over and over, holding her tighter to me.

I look up at Nikolai. "I need to take her to the hospital." She needs help. She needs it now.

He looks back at me with hesitation. That's something the mob doesn't do. At the hospital they ask questions. Questions are something for snitches.

I grind my teeth. I'm not going to let her go without a fight.

"I'm done with this shit, Nikolai." I nearly spit my words out. I look up at him, holding my girl closer to me.

He's the only one I had in my life for the longest time. But that's over now. I'm ready to move on. And this isn't the life I want. It's not the life of a man she deserves. And more than anything, I want to deserve her.

"What's that, Zane? You're done with what?" he asks with a small threat in his voice, but I don't care. I'm not letting go of Maddy, and her and this life simply don't mix.

"I'm out. I don't want this anymore. Take the shop, do what you want. You're the Don now, and I'm asking to go. I'm asking for peace."

Nikolai looks at me and then back at his men. They heard, but they keep their heads down. Nikolai is the boss now. He holds the power.

He takes a few steps back and runs a hand down his face. "Get these fuckers out of here now!" he yells at his men.

"You need to wait till it's clean." I nod and agree, but I don't like it. Nik passes me the plastic wrap and duct tape and it takes me a minute to realize it's for her cut.

I take care of it and keep an eye on her as time passes. I rock her in my arms and watch her breathing. She seems to be doing better and not worse, so that's a good thing.

"She'll be alright," Nik says. I look up at him and his eyes move from her to me. "She's alright."

"I wanna take her to the hospital."

Maddy nestles into my chest, she's quiet and still trembling. This was too much for her.

Nikolai nods his head at me. "Call 'em."

I don't hesitate to reach in my pocket and dial up the ambulance. I'm short and to the point. "I have a young woman in shock on 32 and Sussex." They ask questions that I don't answer. "She needs an ambulance." And with that, I hang up the phone. I may want out of the mob, but I'm sure as shit not going to give them any information.

I'm not a rat.

A long moment passes. "You okay, peaches?" I whisper into Maddy's ear. She nods her head and offers me a small murmur, but her eyes aren't focused.

"What's the shop worth?" Nikolai asks, bringing my attention back to him.

"No clue," I answer him. I don't fucking know. I don't handle the books. "You can check the books."

Nikolai looks at me for a moment. "I'll give you the money, whatever it's worth, and you go where you want." I hold his gaze, feeling a weight lift off my shoulders.

I nod my head as I hear the sirens coming. They're always fast when you hang up.

I don't know why, but it hurts to hear him say that. My eyes water and I'd feel like a little bitch if Nikolai's weren't all glassy-looking, too.

"It's over," he says.

I nod my head and lean down to give Maddy a kiss.

"It's over, baby; we're safe now."

Chapter 26

Madeline

"I think she's awake, Mr. Murphy," I hear Katie say. Her voice sounds muffled, almost as if I'm under water. I hear other people talking too, but their voices are too distorted to understand what they're saying.

Groaning, I struggle to open my eyes. They feel heavy, like they weigh a thousand pounds. On top of that, my body is sore all over and I feel incredibly weak. After a moment, I'm able to lift my eyelids enough to see. Everything is blurry. There are several people, I think, standing over my bed. I blink rapidly to clear my vision, and slowly the room comes into view.

I'm lying in a hospital bed, surrounded by Daddy and Katie. Katie is holding my hand and looking down at me with a mixture of relief and love. Daddy looks like a man who's been told he's won a billion dollar lottery.

As grateful as I am to see these two, I notice one person missing.

Zane, I think with panic. *Where's Zane?*

I try to lift my head to look around, but it's too much for me and I fall back. Seeing my distress, Daddy rushes forward and places a hand on my shoulder to calm me. "I'm here, baby," he reassures me, leaning down to plant a gentle kiss on my forehead. "No one is ever going to hurt you again. I swear it." For a moment, I feel comforted by his words.

"We're both so glad you're alive," Katie adds, her voice filled with joy. She places her hand over her chest. "For a while there, I thought you wouldn't make it. You almost gave your father and I a frickin' heart attack."

I smile briefly at her, so she doesn't think I'm an ungrateful twit. "Where's Zane?" I croak. My voice sounds raw, like I've smoked a hundred packs of cigarettes.

"He had to leave," Katie says, glancing apprehensively at Daddy.

"Why?" I demand, sensing something's not right. Why would he leave me like this?

"Because I told him to," Daddy replies sternly, his smile morphing into a scowl. "I told him to get out and to never come back. He's the reason why you're here, and he can go to hell for it."

Anger swells up from the depths of my stomach. "Why would you do that?" I snap. "Zane saved my life!" I can scarcely remember the events following my rescue, but I clearly remember being held in Zane's loving arms before I lost consciousness. My father was wrong to send Zane away when he'd risked his life to save me.

Daddy snorts. "Saved you? Had you never met the lying bastard, you wouldn't be in this situation."

"I'm only alive because he saved me!" I yell, my voice croaking like a frog. Through the large doorway, I see several nurses stop to stare at me, but I don't give a damn. I'm fucking pissed.

"You have no idea why you're alive," Daddy says. "You're clearly delirious, so I'm going to forgive how you're acting toward me."

"I am not delirious. As soon as they say I'm well enough, I'm out of here! And the first thing I'm going to do is find Zane to tell him how much I love him."

Daddy's face turns red with fury. "You're going to do no such thing, young lady!"

I glare back at him, pretending not to notice Katie fidgeting and looking uncomfortable. I know she must feel pretty conflicted right now, stuck between her best friend and her well-meaning father. "I'm a grown woman. You can't tell me what I can or can't do!"

Daddy glowers at me, the veins standing out his neck. I swear if I wasn't already half-dead, he'd strike me. He takes a deep breath, as if to calm himself and opens his mouth to speak. "You know--"

"Mr. Murphy," Katie says, quietly interrupting him. "I think Maddy and I need a second alone."

Daddy turns on Katie, and at first I think he's going to cuss her out, but he just stares at her.

"Please?" Katie pleads. "Just a few minutes, and I'll let you take the helm."

Daddy turns his gaze back on me for a long moment before grudgingly saying, "Alright. You have five minutes." Not saying another word, he bends down and kisses me on the forehead, and then he walks out of the room, gently closing the door behind him.

"What happened?" I ask her as soon as the door clicks shut. Katie grabs a chair from the corner of the room and drags it over to the bed. She sits down and takes my hand.

"Are you okay?" she asks, her eyes filled with concern.

I shake my head, tears welling up into my eyes. "No," I sigh. "I'm not." Tears roll down my face as I relive the trauma of my kidnapping, and it's an effort to wipe them away. "I need Zane," I say.

Seeing my distress, tears well up in Katie's eyes. "Oh Maddy," she sighs. "I can't imagine what you went through."

My throat feels like it has a lump the size of a bowling ball in it. "They were going to..." I can hardly get the words out. "Rape me... and kill me." I'm grateful my father isn't in here to hear this part of my story. I fear he might blame Zane and go find him and shoot him.

Katie places a hand over her mouth in horror. "Oh God, Maddy, no."

I nod. "It was so awful, Katie. I didn't know if I was going to live or die."

"And Zane really saved you?" she asks in wonder.

"Yes," I reply. "Against all odds, he found me. And then he killed them. He saved me."

Katie's eyes go wide with shock. "He killed the guys who kidnapped you?"

I nod. "And they fucking deserved it," I snarl, half-rising in the bed, my eyes blazing with hatred. "They deserved to be fucking dead!"

Katie's taken aback by the venom in my voice and the savage scowl on my face. I know she thinks that this behavior isn't like me, but she wasn't there. She didn't live through the horror like I did.

"When was Zane last here?" I ask, looking all around as if he's about to pop out of thin air.

"Yesterday, when you were admitted. He called me and told me to get your dad. I did, and then when I got here he told me you had been kidnapped, but everything was fine now. He didn't say anything about killing anybody, though." She bites her lower lip anxiously.

"He didn't tell you because he didn't want Daddy to know.

Daddy hates him, so imagine if he knew what Zane did, even if it was to save me."

"He'd arrest him."

I nod. "Exactly. So I need you to promise me, Katie. Promise me you won't tell a soul about what I've told you."

Katie is a long time in responding, and I fear she's going to run out and tell my father, but finally she nods. "I promise, Maddy. You don't have to worry. I won't tell a soul." She bites her lower lip again and then looks anxious. "But there's something you need to know."

I hold back a groan. I've had enough surprises to last me a lifetime.

"The cops interviewed your dad and me, and I'm sure they're going to interview you as soon as they think you're well enough."

"Ugh," I groan. "That's the last thing I need right now."

"You're going to have to lie to them, Maddy."

"I know that."

"That's making a false statement, and if you ever have to testify in court, you'll be committing perjury."

"I don't give a fuck." I don't care what crime I'll commit by covering for Zane, I'm going to stand by him until the very end.

"Just making sure you know that."

"Thank you," I say sarcastically.

Katie scowls. "Bitch."

I don't miss a beat. "Ho."

Katie laughs and leans down to hug me. "Maddy, I'm just so happy you're alive!"

I wish I could rejoice with her, but I feel sick to my stomach. "Damn, I really wish there was a way I could get out of being interrogated."

"You know, you don't have to talk to them at all, right? You're the victim in this, you can stall them by saying you're not ready to talk about it. And then when you are well enough, you can lawyer up first before saying anything, if you have to say anything at all."

"I'll just say I don't remember shit, that I fell and hit my head, which I did, and I'm having trouble recalling anything." They can't make me talk.

"You always were sort of brain-damaged," Katie agrees, and we both laugh.

"Do you really love him?" Katie asks me in a serious tone after a moment of silence.

"Yes," I reply with conviction. "I do. I don't know if he loves me, or if he and my father will ever get along, but I do love him. Very much."

Katie looks at me with a proud gleam in her eye. "That's good, Maddy. I'm so happy for you, and I'm glad to know you've finally given a man your heart." Then she wryly adds, "Even if he had to murder two guys to capture it."

"Katie!" I protest.

"Wha? You know I'm just pulling your leg. You know, I

talked to Needles too, during all this."

"What did he say?" I ask.

"He told me that they're moving shop. That Zane's out of the mob for good and moving on. When you're well enough, if you still want, I'll take you to Zane."

My eyes brim over with tears. "Thank you so much, Katie."

She rubs my arm affectionately. "That's what friends are for."

I feel so much love and appreciation for Katie right now. She's been my rock throughout my life, and I'm honored that she's going to stand by me and my decision to cover for Zane. I'm not even worried that she'll ever talk about what I've shared with her.

Still there is one last thing that is bothering me. "Katie, am I wrong?" I have to ask. "Zane killed those people, and I'll have to live with that knowledge for the rest of my life. But even knowing that, I still love him and want to be with him. Do you think that makes me a bad person?"

Katie snorts with derision. "I think you refusing to tell me how big Zane's dong is makes you a bad person."

"Katie!"

Katie laughs, and a moment later, I'm laughing right along with her. We laugh and laugh until our sides hurt. When we're done, Katie's expression turns serious and she grabs my hand and rubs it. "No, I don't think you're a bad person, Maddy. You're the best friend a girl could ever ask for."

"Thank you." My eyes well up with tears, and I'm truly

touched. I know then that Katie and I will be friends for life. Our bond is stronger than ever.

Katie smiles at me with great affection, the same that I feel in my heart. "Besides, you can't help who you love."

Grinning and filled with happiness, I squeeze her hand and reply, "Truer words have never been spoken."

Chapter 27

Zane

"You sleep at all last night, man?" Needles asks as I place the machine in the cardboard box as carefully as I can.

"No." I don't mean to be short. But I'm worried about her, and tired as fuck. I stayed up in the waiting room downstairs.

I just can't get the image of her tied up and helpless out of my head. I wish they were alive so I could kill them again. I never wanna leave her side ever again.

I know she left me. I know this shit is my fault. But I couldn't leave her. I respected her father's wishes, but I wasn't going to leave.

The nurse on duty was nice enough to keep me posted. I know she's awake now. I know she's alright. I keep checking my phone, thinking she'll call me. But nothing yet.

I wouldn't even be here if Nikolai hadn't told me the shop needed to be cleared out today.

"It's gonna be alright." Needles slaps my back and gives me a reassuring look. He has no fucking clue how I feel though.

"As soon as this shit is packed up, I'm going back to her. Her father can't stay in that room forever." I don't know if she'll want me. But I have to try.

"Even if he does, so what?" Needles says with a scrunched nose. "Fuck him."

I give him a sad smile. I thought about just being an ass and refusing to leave. But he's her father, and I know she doesn't want us fighting.

"It'll hurt her," I tell him. I know she didn't like it when we fought before. Who am I to go in there causing problems when she's recovering from that shit? The shit I caused her.

I want her though. I need her.

I have to try.

I breathe out deep and get back to loading my shit into cardboard boxes.

I hear the door open behind us and I assume it's Trisha. She's got a box in the back that she needs to move to the new place.

But then I hear Katie's sarcastic mouth. "You better not be leaving town."

I clench my jaw and try to hold in everything I wanna say. I need to know how my girl is. I wanna tell Katie there's no fucking way I'm leaving her. Instead I slowly turn around, and I'm speechless.

Maddy's standing there with a bandage on her leg and a bruise on her face. Her gorgeous green eyes are staring at me with so many emotions shining through.

I drop the shit in my hands and stare back at her, taking her in. I wanna run to her, take her in my arms, and kiss her. I'd drop to my knees and promise to make it up to her. I'd spend the rest of my life doing it.

She looks so uneasy. Like she doesn't know why she's here. Fuck it!

I only have one life to live, and I wanna spend it with her.

I take large strides across the room to take her in my arms. And thank fuck she wraps her arms around me in return. I bury my head in the crook of her neck and kiss every inch available.

"I'm so sorry, Maddy."

She doesn't say anything which makes me nervous, but she holds me tighter.

"Is it true?" she asks in a voice that tells me she's scared to know the answer.

"Is what true?" I pull away and search her eyes. My heart races with panic.

"Are you done with that? All of that?" she asks me. I slowly nod my head as I realize what she's asking.

"I am. It's over. I swear to you."

I hear her sob, and it breaks my heart. I brush her tears

away with my thumb and hold her face in my hands.

"I'm sorry, peaches. I'm so fucking sorry." I take her lips with mine and kiss her with all the passion I have for her. I want her to feel it, and to know it, never doubting me again.

"I'll make it up to you," I whisper with my forehead resting against hers. "Every day for the rest of my life." I kiss her again and she leans into my touch. My hand splays across her back and braces her against me. I don't want to ever let go.

"I love you, Zane." She whispers her words and my heart swells in my chest, but I'm still worried. I wait for a "but". After a moment she pulls back and looks at me, her eyes searching my face and then I see her vulnerability.

She's just waiting for me to say it back.

"I love you too, peaches. Forever."

Chapter 28

Madeline

"Yes!" I scream out as pounds into me. Fuck, he feels so good. Every time is like the first time. He groans in the crook of my neck.

"That's right, peaches," he says as his callused thumb presses against my clit, and I fall hard against the bed. My back bows, and my pussy spasms with an intense orgasm.

"Cum on my dick, baby." He continues fucking me through my release as waves and waves of heated pleasure light every nerve ending on fire.

He thrusts into me, forcing the headboard to bang repeatedly against the wall.

The haze of lust clears for only a moment.

I push up against the wall as if I could stop it, but it's useless. Zane is lost in pleasure and overpowers me, caging me in and fucking me as though he needs his release more than his last breath.

"Fuck!" I scream out as the waves dim and the tips of my toes and fingers tingle. Again. Slight fear overwhelms me as my body heats. My head thrashes, and I try to push him away.

I almost say the words, *I can't*. But Zane's lips find mine. He kisses me with such passion, I'm forced to give myself to him.

His hips pound against mine, each time pushing against my throbbing clit, once, twice, three times and he explodes in me. The feel of his massive cock pulsing inside of me sends me over the edge again.

And we find our release together.

After a moment, my breathing evens and Zane pulls out of me. I wince from how sore I am. We finally moved in together, seriously this time. Not just one of us staying at the other's place. No more roommates. Just us. And he's taken advantage. Not that I'm complaining.

Shit! The headboard.

I peek up at the wall and cover my face.

"Damn it, Zane," I groan into my hands.

"What?" he asks all innocent-like. He knows what he did. He hasn't even sanded the spackle from the last time he dented the wall.

"We need a new headboard." I concede. I fucking love

this one. It's beautiful. But Zane is a beast, and there's no way this is going to work.

He chuckles, all rough and low. And sexy as sin. My clit throbs, and my legs scissor. I can't get enough of him.

"Already?" he says and grins. "You're insatiable." I playfully push him away as he tries to crawl on top of my body.

I giggle and lie on my side, facing him.

I was so scared only weeks ago that we were ruined. That everything that'd happened was just too much. I didn't think our relationship would survive.

Especially when my father came over and saw us together on the sofa. I stood up, ready to tell him not to say anything, but Zane and him took it outside.

I'd be lying if I said I didn't eavesdrop.

My heart nearly leapt up my throat when I heard Zane tell him he killed the men who put their hands on me. He told him everything.

My father still isn't sure that I should be with him, but at least he has some respect for my decision to stay with him and he keeps his mouth shut when he sees him.

The truth is, I needed Zane, and he needed me.

Without each other, we wouldn't have healed like we did. My fingers trace the snake on his arm. It's my favorite thing to do while we're in bed.

"When are you gonna let me give you a tattoo?" he asks me.

I've been thinking about that a lot lately. We have a fresh

start. A new home all to ourselves. I want everyone to know I'm his. I'd be proud to wear his art.

But I'd be prouder to wear something else.

"When you put a ring on it."

He gives me a panty-melting smirk and crawls on top of me. "Is that so?" he asks, cocking a brow and chuckling.

"Hell yeah. Haven't you heard the song, if you like it you shoulda…" My voice trails off as

he reaches over to the nightstand.

Oh hell no. No. He. Did. Not.

He pulls the drawer open and pulls out a small black velvet box.

I cover my mouth with both my hands as tears well in my eyes.

"Madeline Murphy, be my wife." He doesn't ask, of course. I roll my eyes and sniffle before letting out a small laugh.

"You didn't even ask." I look into his eyes and feel so freaking loved.

"Last time I asked you for something, you gave me the runaround for weeks." My shoulders shake with a soft giggle, and my eyes go glassy with tears. "I wasn't willing to take the risk this time."

"I fucking love you, Zane." I wrap my arms around his neck and kiss him with every ounce of passion I have.

He looks into my eyes and smiles wide as he says, "I love you too, peaches."

Epilogue

Zane

"Are you sure it's not going to hurt?" Maddy asks me again. I've told her it's gonna fucking hurt. Tattooing over any bone isn't a walk in the park. But somehow she keeps getting it in her head that I've told her it isn't going to hurt.

"Just a little, but don't worry, I'll make it up to you."

She looks up at me warily and takes in a deep breath. "Alright. Let's do this."

She opens the door to the new shop and walks right in like she owns the place. And I guess she does, since what's mine is hers, now that we're married.

"Hey Needles, do you guys have cosmos here?" she asks Needles, and I can't help but laugh as he gives her a look like she's crazy.

He looks past her and right at me. "She for real, bro?" he asks.

"Give her what she wants, man. She's getting my mark on her."

Needles gives her a big smile and Trisha walks out from the back. She must've heard us come in.

"I got something in the back you'll like." She grins at Maddy, and I get the sense that the two of them have talked about this before.

"Whatever you're drinking, take it down fast, baby." I pull her into my arms and hold her tight to me. "I've been waiting for this for a long time."

"What'd you decide on?" Needles asks Maddy.

She looks back at me with a small smile and then to him and says, "I told him whatever he wants. I trust him." That's almost true. She told me she wanted peaches. Her confession nearly knocked me on my ass.

She said she needed it. She needed me to make my nickname for her permanent, so she can't run from it.

I think I'm going to throw in some sunflowers too. She lights up every time I get them for her now. If she's having a bad day it's real easy to put a smile on her face and then take her to bed and help her forget whatever's bothering her.

Needles snorts a laugh as Maddy pulls away from me and grabs a small pink bottle of something from Trisha. "Well, it's your funeral," he says under his breath.

"Kinky?" Maddy asks.

"Fucking delicious," Trisha says, shooting back her own tiny ass bottle.

"You on the clock?" I ask her.

"Nah, me and Katie are going out tonight."

Maddy rolls her eyes and sets her empty bottle down. "Don't let her get you into trouble."

"Us?" she asks. "Never."

I pull Maddy into the back as I nod to Trisha and Needles. "See you guys later."

She squeezes my hand and takes a deep breath as she sits on the surgical table.

I decide to give her a little laugh. She's too stiff, too worked up.

"How about on your inner thigh? Right near your pussy. Since it's so fucking sweet."

She smiles a bit and bites down on her lip, but she's still nervous.

"You don't have to do this, you know?" I've given her so many chances to back out of this. I know she's not into getting a tat herself. I wouldn't blame her if she never got one. I've been trying to hide my excitement just in case she did want to back out.

She shakes her head emphatically and says, "I want this, Zane."

She lifts her shirt and leans back on the table.

"Make me yours forever," she says.

I bend down and kiss her stomach. Faint stretch marks are still there from when she carried our little man, Gabe. He's safe at home napping with the sitter while we go on our first "date" out. She could do anything she wanted, and this is what she picked.

She took a chance on me. She loved me, married me, and gave me a family.

I look into her gorgeous green eyes and know I'm cherished.

"You are mine forever." I wait for her to look up at me before I say, "I love you, peaches."

She gives me a sweet smile and says, "I love you too, Zane."

About the Authors

Thank you so much for reading our co-written novel. We hope you loved reading it as much as we loved writing it!

For more information on the books we have published, bonus scenes and more visit our websites.

More by Willow Winters
www.willowwinterswrites.com/books

More by Lauren Landish
www.laurenlandish.com

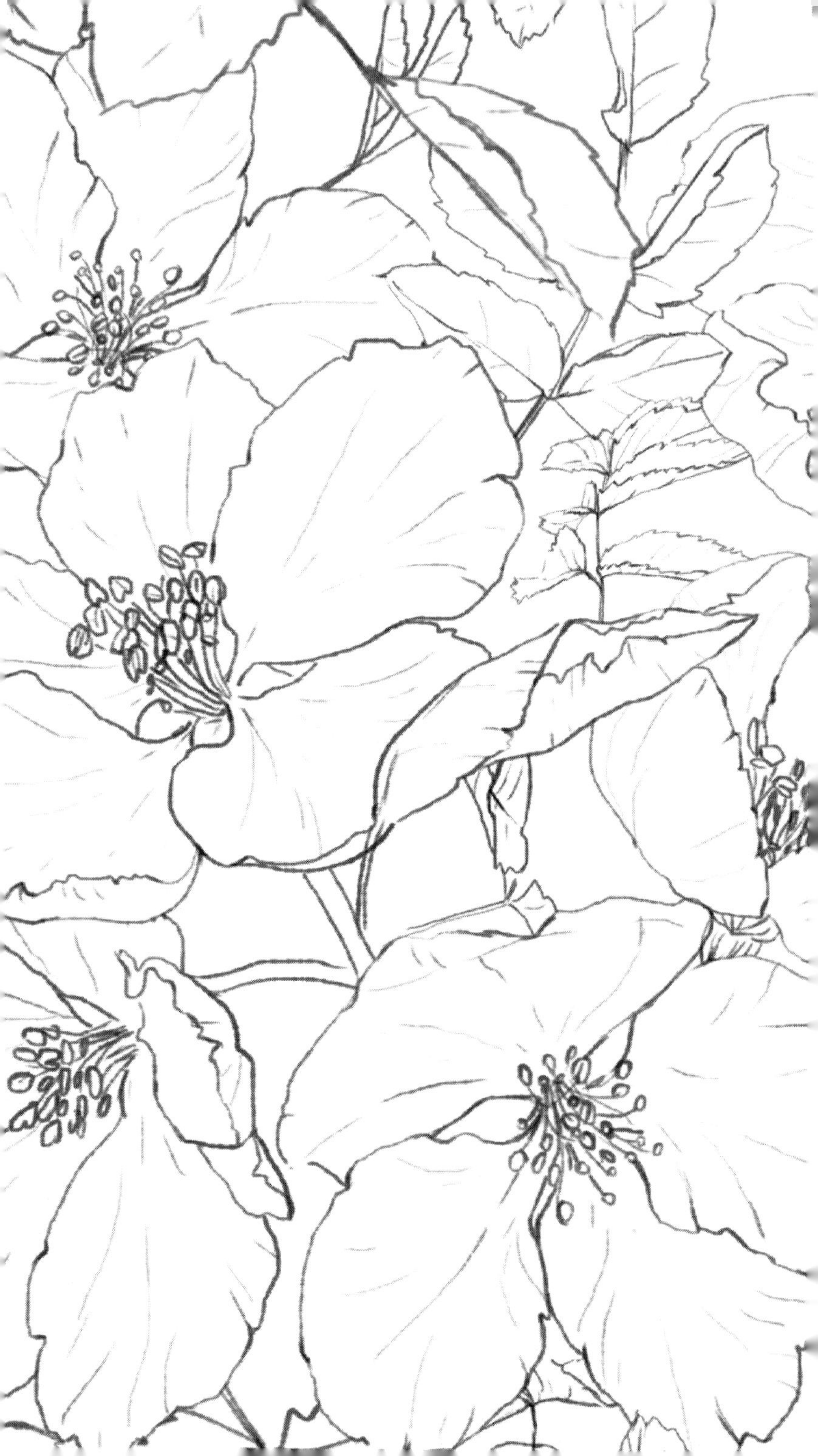

Made in the USA
Middletown, DE
13 January 2022